Story of the Year

the ten winning stories

INDEPENDENT

Story of the Year

★

the ten winning stories

Jane Bates, Andy Blackford, Sara Carroll,
Evelyn Goldsmith, M.L. Greenall,
Dan Jones, Kate Scarratt, Nadya Smith,
Judith Wavell, Malcolm Yorke.

The Federation of Children's Book Groups

SCHOLASTIC

Scholastic Children's Books,
Commonwealth House, 1–19 New Oxford Street,
London WC1A 1NU, UK
a division of Scholastic Ltd
London ~ New York ~ Toronto ~ Sydney ~ Auckland

Published in the UK by Scholastic Ltd, 1997

ISBN 0 590 19961 7

Typeset by DP Photosetting, Aylesbury, Bucks.
Printed in the UK by Clays Ltd, St. Ives plc.

2 4 6 8 10 9 7 5 3 1

Contents

Introduction

It's Story of the Year time again! The *Independent* and Scholastic Children's Books are proud to present 1997's ten best stories for six to nine-year-olds!

The Story of the Year Competition has now been going for five years, and we're very pleased to say that there's been no let-up in the quantity or the quality of the over two thousand entries this year.

These stories were narrowed down to one hundred and eighty, then to twenty-one, and then, hardest of all – to the brilliant final ten we have here. We asked seven distinguished judges to fulfil this tough and soul-searching task – Wendy Berliner, *Independent* Education Editor;

David Fickling, Publishing Director of Scholastic Children's Books; Colin Hughes, Deputy Editor of the *Independent*; Anne Marley, Librarian; Sandi Toksvig, actor and writer; John Walsh, Senior Features Writer for the *Independent*; and Alison Dick of the Federation of Children's Book Groups – an organisation to promote interest and enjoyment in children's books and reading. She represented the children in the voting – pupils from ten schools read the shortlisted stories and their votes were instrumental in the final outcome. Every one of these people – the seven judges and the many children involved – had their say, and eventually the final ten emerged, shining brightly as winners!

And here they are. They're all brilliant! Each one, in its own special way, reflecting the importance of story-telling. There's such a wonderful array of writers here, some new, some established, representing their personal styles and concerns. The two runners-up are fantastic in totally different ways – the hilarious, non-stop action of *Harry the Street Pigeon*; and the gritty, thought-provoking *Joe and the Lion*. The winner is a perfectly rounded, gently funny story which is going to appeal to all readers – children *and* adults – *Spare Bear* by Andy Blackford. But that's not all. From Hallowe'en horror to banyan trees and tigers; from imprisoned poets to bad jokes and football – all of human life is here. And every story has been brought to life, as ever, by a wonderful set of illustrations by top children's illustrators.

So treat yourself to ten great reads!

Scholastic Children's Books

Winner

Spare Bear

ANDY BLACKFORD

Illustrated by
IAN BECK

For Verona and for Sandra

H enry and Susie Dawkins were very careful parents.

When Molly was born, they bought two dummies – an everyday dummy and a spare dummy.

When they lost the everyday dummy, or left it behind, Susie would smile and say, "Don't panic! There's always the spare dummy."

And Henry would sigh and say, "Thank heavens for that. So long as we don't lose the *spare* dummy."

When Molly was older, they bought her a bottle for her milk. They bought her a spare bottle, too, in case they lost the everyday bottle or left it behind.

Once, when they were halfway up the motorway,

Susie cried, "We've forgotten Molly's bottle!"

Henry smiled. "Don't panic. There's always the spare bottle."

But Susie groaned, "I left the spare bottle at Granny's."

"Aha!" said Henry. "Don't panic! I bought a *spare* spare bottle."

"My hero!" laughed Susie.

When Molly was older still, Henry and Susie decided to buy her a new toy.

Said Susie, "She's never had a real teddy bear. Not a big furry one, anyway."

There were lots of bears to choose from at the toy shop. But Henry and Susie only liked two. They were exactly the same, and they sat together on the shelf like twins.

One bear whispered to the other, "They're going to buy me. I can tell."

"I hope so," said the other bear sadly. "Good luck!"

"Let's have one of those," said Henry.

"No," said Susie. "Let's have *two*."

"Why do we want two teddy bears?" asked Henry.

"One for everyday," replied Susie, "one for spare."

The everyday bear was called Bear. Wherever Molly went, Bear went too. When Molly went to bed, so did Bear. When Molly had her bath, Bear sat on the stool beside her. When Molly went out in the car, she sat in her special seat and Bear sat on her lap.

Molly loved Bear so much, she never let him out of her sight. He was never lost or left behind. So there wasn't any need for a spare bear.

Henry and Susie soon forgot about him. He just sat in a cupboard in the dark, day after day, with nothing to do and no one to talk to.

He didn't even have a name. He was just the spare bear.

One day, Susie opened the cupboard door. Spare Bear was excited. He thought, At last Molly needs me!

But Susie was only looking for Molly's hot-water bottle. When she found it, she shut the cupboard door again. But not quite. She left a little gap. And for the first time, Spare Bear could see into Molly's room.

Molly was getting ready for bed. She had her dummy in one hand and her bottle in the other. And she was holding Bear tightly under her arm.

Spare Bear was jealous. He thought, What's Bear got that I haven't got? We're exactly the same. In fact, I'm nicer than Bear because I'm still brand new. I've never even been cuddled.

It was the middle of the night. Spare Bear woke with a start. What was that noise? He looked through the crack in the cupboard door. It was Oscar the dog. He was padding around Molly's room.

Then Molly turned over in her sleep. She was having a bad dream. She gave a little cry and then she threw something over the side of the cot on to the floor.

What could it be? Spare Bear could hardly see in the dark. Then he realized. Oh, dear, he thought. It's Bear!

Oscar the dog dashed across the room, grabbed Bear and ran off with him.

When Spare Bear woke up, it was still dark outside. But Susie switched on the light in

Molly's room and started putting her clothes into a suitcase.

Molly was still fast asleep. "Come on, Madam!" said Susie. "Time to get up. We're going to America!"

"The cab's outside," said Henry.

"Final check," said Susie. "Everyday dummy?"

"Here," said Henry.

"Spare dummy?" asked Susie.

"Here," said Henry.

"Everyday bottle?" asked Susie.

"Here," said Henry.

"Spare bottle?" asked Susie.

"Here," said Henry.

"Bear?" asked Susie.

"Uh-oh!" sighed Henry. "No Bear."

Spare Bear watched through the crack in the cupboard door as Henry and Susie pulled the mattress out of Molly's cot. They looked under the bed, under the chair, everywhere. But Bear was nowhere to be found.

In the end, Henry said, "The cab's outside. We'll just have to go."

But Molly cried, "Bear? BEAR? **BEAR?**"

"Oh, no!" said Susie. "This is a nightmare! We can't go to America without Bear!"

Then Henry remembered. "Don't panic! There's always the spare bear!"

Together they shouted, "THE SPARE BEAR!" and they threw open the cupboard door.

The light was so bright, it made Spare Bear blink. Susie grabbed him by the arm and pulled him out of the cupboard. "Come on, Spare Bear!" she said. "You've got a plane to catch!"

What's a plane? Spare Bear wondered.

As they ran from the house to the taxi, Molly cried, "Oscar?"

"Oscar can't come with us, darling," said Susie. "Granny will look after him while we're away."

Spare Bear had a wonderful holiday in America.

He went to the top of the Empire State Building.

He floated down the Grand Canyon in a rubber boat.

And every night, he went to sleep in Molly's arms. He had never been so happy in all his life.

The only time he felt sad was when Molly called him Bear. Then he would think, I shouldn't be here at all. If Molly found out I wasn't Bear, she wouldn't love me any more.

Something else worried Spare Bear. Soon it would be time to go home. Then what would happen? Would he have to go back in the cupboard? How he'd miss Molly, he thought. He'd be so lonely without her.

It was time to say goodbye to America. As their plane rose into the sky over New York, Molly and Spare Bear waved to the Statue of Liberty.

Granny and Oscar were waiting at the airport to meet them. Spare Bear's heart was pounding in case Bear was there, too. But he wasn't.

By the time they got home, it was dark and Molly was nearly asleep. Susie carried her up to bed and tucked her in with Spare Bear.

Still no sign of Bear. As he dozed off, Spare Bear didn't feel quite so worried.

Next morning, he was woken by a snuffling and a wuffling. Molly was awake, too. She was sitting up in bed, pointing with both hands at some-

thing. "Bear!" she shouted. "Oscar! **BEAR!**"

Poor Spare Bear hardly dared look.

But there was Oscar, holding a very wet, muddy bear in his mouth.

Then in came Henry, still half-asleep. When he saw Oscar, he froze. "Susie! Come and see this!"

Susie couldn't believe her eyes. "It's Bear! Oscar must have buried him in the garden!"

"Woof!" said Oscar. He was very pleased with himself.

Susie rescued Bear from the dog's mouth. "Nothing wrong with *him* that a good old wash won't cure."

"Bear!" gurgled Molly. "Bear!"

Spare Bear thought his heart would break. They would put him back in the cupboard, now. No more cuddles. No more holidays.

But Henry said, "I think we should clean up the old bear and keep *him* as a spare."

This can't be true! thought Spare Bear. I must be dreaming!

"Good idea," said Susie. "Molly loves the new bear. She might as well hang on to him."

Spare Bear was so happy, he could have

danced. But later, when Molly was downstairs having her breakfast, he began to feel guilty.

This isn't fair on poor Bear, he thought. It wasn't his fault the dog got him. And while I was having fun on holiday, he was buried in the garden. And now they're going to put him away in the cupboard.

No. It's just not fair.

Spare Bear knew what he had to do. He crept out of Molly's cot and crawled under the wardrobe. He found the darkest, dustiest corner and curled up in a ball. "Oh, well," he sighed. "Alone again." Two big tears rolled down his furry cheeks. "Oh, well."

He wasn't sure how long he'd been hiding when he heard Molly cry, "Bear!" She was upset. "BEAR!"

Susie was trying to calm her. "It's all right, darling! Look, here's Bear. He was very dirty. Mummy had to wash him. But now he's lovely and clean for you."

"**BEAR!**" yelled Molly.

"Henry! Have you seen the new bear? I've looked everywhere."

"I'm afraid not. Last time I saw him, he was in the cot."

"Strange," said Susie. "Listen, Molly, this is the *real* Bear. He's come back!"

"**BEAR, BEAR, BEAR!**" screamed Molly.

"It's no good, Henry, she's in a state. She wants the new bear. I don't know what to do with her."

Under the wardrobe, there was a snuffling and a wuffling. It was too dark to see anything, but Spare Bear felt a cold, wet nose rubbing his face.

"Woof!" Oscar's bark nearly deafened Spare Bear. "Woof! Woof!"

"Look!" he heard Henry say. "Oscar's found something!"

Oscar grabbed Spare Bear around the middle and dragged him out into the light.

"It's the new bear! Clever boy, Oscar!"

"Woof!" replied Oscar, very pleased with himself.

Now Molly was laughing through her tears. "*Two* Bear, Mummy! *Two* Bear!"

"That's it!" cried Henry. "She wants *both* bears!"

* * *

And so began a long and happy life together for Molly, Bear and Two Bear (not Spare Bear, because he wasn't spare any more).

The bears became the best of friends and Molly took them everywhere.

One day, Henry put down his paper and took off his glasses. "Susie, have you ever wondered what we'd do if one of the bears got lost, or accidentally left behind?"

"I know," she said. "It worries me, too."

"Maybe," said Henry, "maybe we should buy a *spare* bear..."

"Maybe we should buy *two*," said Susie.

ANDY BLACKFORD

Andy Blackford was born in Middlesbrough and now lives in London. He has three children – Tom (fifteen), Nick (twelve), and Verona (two). He is a member of the British Sub-Aqua Club and worked as a professional guitarist, a journalist and a creative director in advertising before applying himself full-time to writing. He is the author of five published works, including the history of the nightclub, the authorized biography of Tyneside rock legends, The Animals, and a collection of humorous essays on diving. He also enjoys endurance running and recently ran across the Sahara in le Marathon des Sables, generally accepted to be the world's toughest foot race.

He says: "I began writing stories for children with the birth of my daughter. The prospect of having to read and re-read the same bland and formulaic books for years loomed over me like a jail sentence.

"Unlike the toy market, kids' books are not the subject of 'pester power'. The poor old parent has to choose, as well as buy the product, and is then condemned to live with that purchase decision until the audience nods off.

"Authors should at least have the good grace and common humanity to provide some light relief for Mum and Dad."

Runner-up

Joe and the Lion

NADYA SMITH

Illustrated by
NICK SHARRATT

For Christopher

Joe did not want a birthday party. "Nobody'll come," he told his mother. "Even if I tell them there'll be presents they won't come."

His mother (who knew nothing) was puzzled. "Of course they'll come," she insisted. "Everyone loves a party – all your friends— "

"I haven't got any," said Joe.

His mother went to see his teacher. "No friends?" exclaimed Miss Evans (who also knew nothing). "Of course he has friends! You know what eight-year-olds are like – one day they're the best of buddies, the next day they're not speaking to each other, and the day after that they're back together again."

Joe's mother went home comforted. "Miss Evans says you've got lots of friends," she told him.

Joe sighed. "She wouldn't say that if she *knew*."

"Knew what? Tell me."

But Joe wouldn't say. How could his mother or Miss Evans possibly know what went on in the hidden corners of the playground, in the cloakrooms, in the street after school? He wasn't teased and bullied just because he was black. There were plenty of black children in school who did not have a hard time. But to be black *and* small for his age, *and* have matchstick legs, *and* not to be particularly good at anything, *and* have to wear the horrible pullovers that his auntie knitted for him in mustard yellow and then, wear glasses...

"I don't want a party!" he shouted. "Nobody'll come and I won't come either!"

It was Miss Evans' fault that he had to wear the glasses. She had sent a note home to say that she thought he should have his eyes tested. She thought that perhaps poor eyesight might account for the problems he had with reading.

"What problems?" Joe demanded. "I can read."

"I know darling – but this might make such a difference."

Joe was taken to the optician who fitted him with steel-rimmed reading glasses. His mother was delighted. "You look like a professor!" she beamed.

Right. So glasses will make me a genius, thought Joe bitterly.

The first time he took them to school Wayne, the chief among his tormentors, snatched them off his desk.

"Give them back!" shouted Joe. He didn't want them back, but neither did he want the trouble he would be in if he didn't have them.

Wayne put the glasses on. "Ah – perhaps I'll be able to see your legs now, matchsticks!" He peered at Joe. "No. 'Fraid not. Needs a microscope."

"Give them back," Joe pleaded through the shouts of laughter. "My mum'll kill me if they get broken." He made a grab for the glasses but Wayne got there first, snatching them off his nose and holding them behind his back. "Fifty-p tomorrow – and you can have 'em."

"I haven't got 50p!"

"Well get it then."

That evening his mother said, "If you don't want a party we could have a day out. Where would you like to go?"

"Disneyland," Joe said.

"Don't be silly."

"The zoo then. I've never been to a zoo."

"Yes, that's better. We'll go on Saturday and take a picnic."

Joe took a deep breath. "Can I have 50p?"

"What for?"

"Sweets."

"I'm not made of money, Joe – you'll have plenty of sweets when we go to the zoo."

"But—"

"Anyway, they're bad for your teeth." She changed the subject. "How are the glasses? Do they help with reading? Where are they now?"

"They're at school," Joe said. "Miss Evans told me to keep them in my desk."

When Joe got to school, Wayne and his gang were waiting for him in the playground. Wayne was holding a green balloon on a string.

"Got the money?" he demanded.

"Mum wouldn't give it me."

"Mum wouldn't give it me!" mimicked Wayne. "Look, Matchsticks." He held out the balloon and Joe could see that his glasses were tied to the end of the string.

Wayne said, "This is a helium balloon. My sister got it at a party. If I let it go now it'll go right up there," he pointed, "into the clouds." The children sniggered.

Joe struggled against impending tears. There was no way he was going to cry in front of Wayne. "Give them to me," he managed to say.

"No 50p?" said Wayne. "Well, you can have them after the weekend. On Monday. For a fiver. Otherwise..." He glanced at the sky. "Up, up, and away."

A fiver! Five pounds! Wayne might just as well have said five hundred. But if he didn't get it... Joe could picture the glasses sailing into the sky – getting smaller and smaller and smaller until they vanished altogether.

The next day was Saturday. Joe was nine years old. He had hoped for a Game Boy but what he got was a watch, a box of Lego pieces which he could build into a helicopter, and some Star Trek figures. He reckoned that his mum must have spent at least fifteen pounds and wished that he could have had the money instead.

The zoo cost four pounds fifty for his mother and two pounds for him. "That's a lot of money just to look at a few animals," said his mother, scratching about in her purse. "But never mind – it is your birthday."

"I don't mind not going," Joe said quickly. "I could have some money instead..."

"Nonsense. We're here now, and we've got our lunch with us. We won't have to spend anything else."

They saw the elephants, the giraffes, the monkeys and the crocodiles. They watched the seals catching fish thrown by a keeper, and stared in horror as a snake feasted on a dead mouse. All the time, at the back of Joe's mind was the picture of the green balloon soaring into the sky and carrying his glasses – who knows where?

And then ... he saw the lion. It lay pressed

against the bars of the cage, its massive, honey-coloured paws stretched out in front, its head facing away so that the thick, matted hair of its mane tumbled through the bars. Everything about it was huge and powerful – from the bulging muscles at its shoulders to the thick, black-tufted tail.

There was a barrier round the cage so that no one could get near, but Joe ran to it and leaned over as far as he could. As he did so, the lion turned its head and gazed at him with its yellow eyes. Joe saw the pale eyelashes, the pink, moist triangle of the nose, the white beard below black, shiny lips. He was stunned by the strength and beauty of the creature. So still and yet so strong! Nobody would ever dare—

"You like lions then?"

A man, black like himself, was leaning on the barrier beside him.

Joe nodded. "Mustn't speak to strangers" came automatically into his head, but he looked round and saw his mother inspecting some fancy birds in a nearby enclosure, so he reckoned it was all right.

"He's – *magic*!"

The man said, "You know, in Kenya – where this lion comes from – a boy would have to go and kill a lion like this before he could become a real man, a warrior. All he had was just a spear. No gun or anything like that."

"I wouldn't want to kill it," Joe said.

"These people believed that if they ate lion meat they would somehow become as strong as the lion. They used to cut out the claws and pull out the teeth to make necklaces. They wore them to make themselves fierce and brave. And they would skin the lion and use the skin as a cloak which would keep them safe from harm."

"Poor lion!" said Joe.

"They can't do that any more," said the man. "It's against the law."

Joe gazed into the shining yellow eyes. If only he could have just a little of that strength! He closed his own eyes and prayed silently to the lion in much the same way as his mother had taught him to pray to God.

I don't want your claws or your teeth or your skin, and I don't ever want to kill you, but please, *please* make me strong and brave!

Make me strong and brave!

He stretched across the barrier towards the bars. Perhaps if he could just touch – but the man caught his wrist and pulled him back. "No, son. Don't do that! Don't even think of it. Nobody touches the lion."

Joe's mother came up. "It's time to go now. Haven't you seen enough of that lion?" She smiled at the man and took Joe's hand.

"What was he saying to you?" she asked as they walked away.

"Nothing really," Joe said. "Just about – well, lions."

Joe's dad came every other Sunday to take him out. Sometimes they would go to the cinema and buy hot dogs and popcorn to eat during the film. At other times his dad would say, "Bring your football, son." Joe had come to know that this meant his dad was skint. They would buy a bag of chips and go to the park. Which was free. But this Sunday, as soon as he opened the front door he said, "Can we go to the zoo, Dad? For my birthday?" He knew his dad would have forgotten – he always did.

His dad wasn't too pleased. He'd planned a

park and chips day. But because he hadn't bought a present for Joe he had to agree.

"But you went yesterday!" exclaimed his mother. "Spent all the time looking at that smelly old lion."

"He wasn't smelly!" cried Joe. "And anyway, he liked me looking at him." Joe's dad had to turn out his pockets to find enough money for the zoo. Joe waited anxiously. No good looking for a fiver *there*, he thought. Tomorrow was Monday. Nightmare day with Wayne waiting in the playground, no fiver, and his glasses sailing into the sky behind a green balloon. He needed to talk to the lion.

As soon as they got inside, he rushed to the cage. It was a warm day and the lion was enjoying the sunshine. It lay on its side, exposing its taut white belly and the strong leathery pads on its hind feet. The shiny black lips seemed to be curved into a smile. Joe leaned on the barrier. His mother had said the lion was smelly – but was it? He gave a long careful sniff – caught a faint, musky perfume, strange and disturbing. He sniffed again, breathing it in, strong ... strong...

Suddenly the lion shifted its head close to the barrier and yawned. A tremendous yawn! Joe found himself staring into the black cavern of its mouth, framed with huge white teeth, a massive fang at each corner, and inside, the dark pink, rasping tongue curling and stretching as though it had a life of its own. And the smell! Fetid, meaty, powerful. Joe breathed in the lion's hot breath – breathed, gasped, choked and breathed again. Filled his lungs with the strength of the lion.

"Thank you, thank you!" he whispered.

It was Monday morning. The day of reckoning. Joe padded into the playground. His head was sunk into his shoulders, rolling slightly as he walked, and his eyes were focused, unblinking, on the crowd of children standing near the far wall. Wayne stood in front, holding the balloon.

"Got the cash?" he yelled.

Joe didn't answer. Through his lion eyes he didn't see children. He saw the tall grasses of the savannah and, in the distance, a herd of zebra or wildebeest or deer. His prey. He padded on,

silent, focused. The children were puzzled. They looked to Wayne for guidance but he was staring uneasily at Joe who continued his measured advance.

"Have you got the cash?" Wayne repeated uncertainly.

Joe had reached him. With one swipe he seized the balloon and burst it with the pin he had ready. Then swiftly moving behind Wayne, he threw his arm round his neck as though to give him an affectionate hug. Then, with a powerful jerk, small as he was, he brought the bigger boy crashing to the ground and held him there, an arm across his throat, a knee in his stomach. With his free hand, he unhurriedly picked up the glasses, folded them and put them in his pocket.

Then he stared at Wayne and opened his lips. From the depths of his belly, up through his chest and rumbling through his throat came a deep and terrible growl.

The children backed away.

"Geroff," said Wayne in a shaky voice. He was scared.

He was so scared he began to cry.

Contemptuously Joe pushed him away and stood up. Wayne scrambled to his feet and fled, followed by the jeers of the other children.

Joe put on his glasses. He raised his clenched fists to the sky – and roared.

Nadya Smith

Nadya Smith lives in Birmingham and has three grown-up sons and three grandchildren. She has worked in a children's hospital, and as a teacher in Birmingham. On retiring from teaching, she participated in Community Literacy Projects, working with Asian women, teaching them English and introducing them to libraries and books for children. She has had two books of stories published for Asian children, as well as contributing to story collections. She has also written several scripts for BBC Schools Radio. She enjoys writing, reading, gardening, music, and being with her family. When she wins the lottery she will travel to New Zealand and India!

She says: "My ambition is to put Asian children into the literary scene. There are so few books which feature urban Asian teenagers and I would love to produce something for twelve to fifteen-year-olds about themselves. Their lives are changing so rapidly – especially for the girls – and the struggle between the demands of their culture and those of their Western education is so dramatic and funny/tragic that it should be recorded."

Runner-up

Harry the
Street Pigeon

M.L. GREENALL

Illustrated by
ANT PARKER

To John

" T ypical! Absolutely typical of human feet! Always flattening your food!" grumbled Harry, as he scraped a squashed chocolate-coated raisin off the pavement with his beak. Harry was a London pigeon and he lived on the bits of food people dropped as they passed by in the street. He flew back up to the gutter which was his home above a sweet shop, and thought crossly about feet.

"It's always the best bits they tread on, too. Flat chips! Flat popcorn! Flat peanuts! Flat raisins!" Raisins were Harry's favourite food, and a rare treat. "It would be nice to have one that wasn't squashed flat for a change. How would humans like it if I trod all over *their* food?"

Just then the morning breeze blew across the gutter, carrying with it all the smells of the street.

The breeze was like a newspaper to Harry, and he read it every day for new smells. There were all the usual ones – tomatoes and olives from the pizza takeaway, onions and chips from the burger restaurant, coffee from the supermarket – but there were some different ones, too. Old socks, was it? No, not socks, but a fancy cheese at the delicatessen. There was a strong whiff of flea-powder on that snooty Afghan hound passing by on a lead, and there were fresh tulips in the flower shop. And hang about! Wasn't that cake? Not just any old stuff, but top quality cake with loads of raisins and currants, and chocolate and marzipan. A new cake shop must have opened!

I'm off to investigate. There may be some crumbs I can pick up before they all get trodden on, thought Harry.

He flew down the street, past the cinema and the supermarket, and the TV rental shop, and the hairdresser's shop where a fat woman sat, looking very silly, with pieces of tinfoil in her hair. The smell of cake was growing stronger all the time.

"This is it!" cried Harry suddenly. "And yet it

can't be! This is the shop which sells pretty ornaments!" The shop door was wide open, and the most beak-watering smells came from inside. Puzzled, Harry flew on to the shop's broad window-ledge for a closer look.

"Blow me down with a feather! Those aren't ornaments, they *are* cakes! But I never realized it before, because this shop door has always been shut so I couldn't smell them."

Written across the window in big gold letters were the words GLORIA GOODBODY'S GATEAUX, but Harry couldn't read, and anyway he didn't know gateaux was French for cakes.

He stared through the window admiringly. The centre-piece was a chocolate sponge Noah's Ark with Mr and Mrs Noah standing on deck in yellow anoraks and sou'westers. Mr Noah's long white beard was made from icing sugar, and Mrs Noah had two yellow marzipan plaits peeping out below her sou'wester. Behind the Noahs were pairs of marzipan animals. Brightly-coloured fish played in the blue marzipan waves around the Ark, and a white dove sat on the roof with a green twig in its beak.

Another cake was made like a table laid for a birthday party, complete with white tablecloth, little plates and mugs, tiny chocolate éclairs, and even a cake which was a miniature copy of the birthday cake it stood on. Then there was a chocolate thatched cottage with roses growing round the porch, and a marzipan garden full of sugar flowers. And because it was nearly Easter, there were two straw hats which were so realistic you could almost have walked out the shop wearing one, even though they were made from meringue and pastry and syrupy fruit.

But the cake Harry liked most was the one like a green football pitch with a little black and white football in the centre. "Just the right size for a pigeon," he sighed. "How I'd love to kick it into one of those goals like they do on the telly in the TV rental shop."

A woman came out of the shop with a pink cake box tied with gold ribbon. Harry followed her, hoping she would eat the cake in the street and drop some crumbs, as people did when they came out of takeaways, but she carried the box carefully into a taxi. He examined the pavement for crumbs people might have dropped earlier, but there weren't any. It was most disappointing, and the smell of cake was making Harry so hungry.

Harry's mother had taught him never to go into shops or houses because humans were dangerous. But I can handle people, he thought, I'm a street pigeon, aren't I? All you've got to do is watch out for their feet. Why, humans are so stupid they can't even fly!

He took a few cautious steps into the shop. He'd never trodden anywhere so clean in his life. The shiny pink floor felt nice underfoot, but there wasn't a crumb on it anywhere. Two young women in pink pinafores and frilly caps stood chatting behind the counter. They were too deep in conversation to notice Harry.

"It's bloomin' cold with that door open, Hayley," said one.

"I know, Linda," replied Hayley, "but Mrs Goodbody says we must leave it open so the smell of cakes will attract people into the shop."

"I feel ever so silly wearing vanilla essence behind my ears," said Linda.

"So do I," agreed Hayley, "but Mrs Goodbody says it will whet people's appetites and make them buy her cakes."

"*Gâteaux*, Hayley, we're supposed to call them *gâteaux*."

"Expensive is what I call them," grumbled Hayley. "You'd think she could pay us higher wages, the prices she charges. She'll be back from the hairdresser's soon. She's always getting her hair done. I wonder what colour it will be this time? Remember when she wanted it mauve, and it came out orange?"

Linda and Hayley giggled so much they didn't see Harry hop up into the window among the cakes.

Harry looked around him and thought, If I take a little peck from each cake no one will ever notice. But first I must have a kick at that football. He stepped on to the green iced cake and kicked the ball as hard as he could. It missed the goal, and caught Mr Noah on the back of his head, sending him toppling overboard into a strawberry-filled heart, where he sank halfway up to his beard in red jam.

"Sorry about that, mate," muttered Harry, wondering where the ball had gone. Then he saw it on top of the meringue of one of the hats. It would be fun to have one more kick, and when Harry landed on the hat he had a nasty surprise. It wasn't smooth and firm like the football pitch, but softer than wet snow, and horribly sticky. His feet went though the meringue and into the lemon filling. He sank down until he could feel the little ball beneath his feet where it had settled firmly on the pastry base, but there was no hope of kicking it out. Harry had never realized food could be so deep. He began to panic, and had quite a struggle to get himself out of the hat; and by then it didn't look like a hat any more.

There was a sponge teddy bear in chocolate sunglasses, sunbathing on its back on a little blue and white striped icing-sugar towel. Harry tried to clean up his sticky feet by wiping them on the bear's tummy, but he scuffed up a lot of crumbs, and the bear looked as if it was moulting. Harry ate some of the crumbs to tidy it up, but the bear only looked worse.

Harry soon discovered that some cakes were firm, and others were slippery and gooey. He had a bad moment sliding down the roof of the thatched cottage. It was made of chocolate-butter icing, and his feet left two deep grooves behind him as he slithered off it. He accidentally pulled away the porch and the rambling roses, before landing on the sugar flowers in the marzipan garden and smearing them all with chocolate. Then he hopped on to the cake like a birthday party table, and left chocolate foot-prints all over it, after pecking some experi-mental holes. Sponge again! *Where* were the currants and raisins? He could smell them close by.

Right at the back of the display, he spotted a cake shaped like an igloo, and knew at once. "That's where the currants and raisins are – inside it!"

An eskimo with a harpoon stood at the igloo's entrance. Harry didn't like the look of the har-poon, so he pattered round to the back of the igloo, out of the eskimo's sight. He chipped away some icing, and found cake with as many cur-rants and raisins as any pigeon could wish for. He pecked a hole big enough to get his head inside the igloo, and before he realized it he'd eaten it empty.

"That was lovely!" he sighed. "I don't suppose

the eskimo will mind when he finds out I've eaten the inside of his igloo. More room for *him* now. But I'm so full, I must have a snooze before I fly home." He hopped on to an empty cake-stand, and was asleep in no time.

It was peaceful in the shop. Hayley had gone to the kitchen to fetch a tray of freshly-baked Danish pastries and currant buns, and Linda was leaning against the counter, staring through the open door, day-dreaming. One moment a shop can be quite empty, and the next it is full of people. That's what happened while Harry slept. A little queue formed. Then a woman came in and walked to the head of it. "You won't mind if I'm served first, will you?" she asked the queue. "But I've left my Porsche on a double yellow line."

Some people said they *did* mind, but she ignored them. "I'll have six Danish pastries, six currant buns, and let me see, what else?" She turned to look at the cakes in the window display, and saw Harry dozing on one leg on the cake-stand. "Oh!" she cried. "I must have that *gorgeous* pigeon cake! It's *so* lifelike! Has it got currants and raisins inside?"

Harry was a light sleeper. He woke instantly. "How does she know I've got currants and raisins inside me?" He drew himself up, and flapped his wings at the woman indignantly. She screamed. "Oh! It's real! How horrible! I'm terrified of real birds!" And she fainted face-down on to the tray of warm Danish pastries that Hayley had just put on the table next to the counter.

It was then that Mrs Goodbody returned from the hairdresser. Her hair was raspberry pink and brushed up into big waves, and she strode into the shop looking very large and important in a dress the same colour as her hair. She stopped still suddenly, and demanded: "WHO IS THAT WOMAN ASLEEP ON MY DANISH PASTRIES?"

"I don't know her name," said Hayley, "but she's not asleep. She's fainted. The pigeon done it."

"The pigeon *did* it," corrected Mrs Goodbody.

"That's what I said, Mrs Goodbody. The pigeon done it."

"Pigeon?" boomed Mrs Goodbody. "What pigeon done *what*? I mean—" Then she caught sight of Harry, and anger made her quiver like a raspberry jelly that had been struck with a spoon. "Who let that filthy bird in here?" she gasped.

"It must have flown in," said Hayley. "You told us to leave the door open. You said the smell of baking might get the skinflints round here to open their wallets. You said they were all so stingy—"

Mrs Goodbody's face had turned an ugly red, which clashed with her hair.

"Um. Er, er," she stuttered. "That was just a joke, Hayley."

Some of the customers laughed, and Mrs Goodbody's face went even redder.

"I'm getting that disgusting pigeon out of here. Instantly!" she shouted, and pulled on a pair of the hygienic rubber gloves that Hayley and Linda had to wear when they handled the cakes. She advanced towards Harry with a cake slice in one hand and a pink teacloth in the other.

"Don't hurt it!" said one of the customers.

"Hmmmph!" snorted Mrs Goodbody.

Harry didn't like the look in her eye, nor did he like being called disgusting. He spread his wings wide and flapped them at Mrs Goodbody, hoping to make her faint like the other lady. But Mrs Goodbody didn't faint. She brandished the cake slice menacingly, and snarled, "Just wait till I get my hands on you!"

Not likely, thought Harry – but in his haste to fly off the cake-stand he tipped it over, and it fell against the empty igloo. The icing broke like a china bowl.

"Oh! You've eaten my igloo!" hissed Mrs Goodbody, and then she saw Mr Noah in the strawberry heart, and the grooves in the thatched-cottage roof, and the footprints on the birthday cake, and the ruined meringue hats. "*And where is my football?*" she shouted.

Harry hopped on to the deck of the Ark out of Mrs Goodbody's reach, but his wing caught Mrs Noah off balance, and sent her *plop!* into the strawberry heart beside her husband. They looked quite cosy side by side up to their chests in red jam, but Mrs Goodbody didn't think so.

"My Ark! My gateaux!" she shrieked. "You horrible, revolting bird! Get out of my shop before I murder you!"

Don't worry, I'm going, thought Harry, but in

his haste, he forgot there was a glass window between him and the street, and he flew straight into it. He fell back on to a pair of meringue Easter bunnies who were holding a fragile meringue basket filled with jammy strawberries. Harry flapped so wildly to get back on his feet that the bunnies and their basket were reduced to a blizzard of meringue crumbs, and most of the strawberries were squashed to a pulp.

The flapping roused the woman who had fainted, and she lifted her head in a daze. "Am I in heaven?" she asked Hayley. "I can hear the beat of angels' wings!"

"No, that's just the pigeon," said Hayley, and the woman fainted back on to the Danish pastries again.

The photographer from the local paper dropped into the shop to buy a currant bun for his elevenses. Lucky I've got my camera with me, he thought. Could be a front page picture here. What a mess! That old girl with the raspberry hair looks in a right old temper. I don't fancy the pigeon's chances against *her*.

Mrs Goodbody took a swipe at Harry with the cake slice, and missed. He leapt up in terror and tried to fly over her, but a large strawberry had caught on his claw, and the weight of it forced him to crash-land on her head. Mrs Goodbody wasn't so frightening to Harry now that he couldn't see her angry face. Her hair was still warm from its blow dry, and he found it good for cleaning his sticky feet. He shook the strawberry from his claw, and it slid through Mrs Goodbody's hair and stuck to her eyebrow. Several people laughed, but they tried to make it sound as though they were coughing.

"My hair! My highlights!" Mrs Goodbody screamed.

"Watch the birdie!" said the photographer from the doorway.

Mrs Goodbody made a strangled sound.

"Only joking!" he said, his camera flashing.

"Don't you dare print that photograph!" cried Mrs Goodbody.

"Publicity! Just what you need to send your sales soaring," replied the photographer. "Now give us a smile, darling."

Mrs Goodbody glared.

"Think how light your cakes must be to break so easily," said a customer, encouragingly.

"Think of all the lovely trifle you can make with the broken bits," said another. "Think of all the lovely insurance you can claim!" said the photographer. Mrs Goodbody beamed, and the camera flashed again.

Meanwhile Harry had seen the open doorway. He gave his feet one last wipe on Mrs Goodbody's hair, then spread his wings and flew off into the street. The photographer took a final picture of him, and some of the people in the shop cheered Harry on his way.

That's positively the last time I'm ever eating indoors, thought Harry, as he splashed under the fountain in the square round the corner a few minutes later.

And if there's one thing worse than sticky food, it's *deep* food. Flat food's not so bad after all.

M.L. GREENALL

M.L. is short for Mary Louise, but this author is generally known to her friends as M.L.! She lives mostly in London, but also spends a lot of her time in Cornwall, where her husband, who is a professional painter, likes to draw and paint. M.L. studied pottery at Camberwell Art School, and then became increasingly interested in drawing and painting, showing and selling work in mixed exhibitions, including the Royal West of England Academy and the Royal Academy. She has also had several short stories published in magazines. She is a member of Friends of the Earth, Greenpeace, Amnesty International and the RSPB, and she enjoys photography, gardening and reading.

She says: "I have enjoyed writing since I was seven when I wrote my first story, and was deeply offended when my father read it and fell about laughing. It wasn't meant to be funny. What I particularly like about writing for children is the opportunity to allow my imagination full range in a world of fantasy, but a world which nevertheless must have its own logic. If I get too carried away, the thought of a child critically reading my story over my shoulder makes me stop and wonder, Does this make sense? Can I cut this down? And worst of all, Am I boring you?"

Millie, Man of the Match

JANE BATES

Illustrated by
SAMI SWEETEN

To Tookie and my family, with thanks for all your encouragement

I t's just not worth living, having a sister like mine, thought Matthew, angrily kicking a stone. 6–1. Lost again. And all because of Millie.

As the teams filed into the changing room he watched his twin sister Camilla toss her dark curls and grin at their captain, Dazz, who glared back at her. No one else had a sister in the football team, Matthew thought. Trust it to be him.

It wasn't that Millie couldn't play. On the contrary. She modelled herself on her hero, Liam Stokes, the young City player reckoned to be the next David Beckham. Like Liam, her dribbling was delightful, her passes professional and her headers heavenly. But where Liam played football like a gentleman, Millie went on the pitch like Boadicea in a bad mood. Her tackles were treacherous and her fouls ferocious. She had given away more penalties than she'd had hot dinners.

The score-line would have been rather different without Millie, Matthew said to himself. Six goals minus three penalties would have made it 3–1. Except that Millie had scored their only goal.

They trudged home in silence, Millie with that infuriating smile of hers, and Matthew with a face as long as a month of wet Sundays. He had to live down another defeat. The other boys would get him Monday morning, he knew.

"We ought to have two baths in this house!" said Matthew's mum, when they got home. "You can't come in the house like that! Matthew, you sit and wait on the doorstep while Camilla has first bath, and you can go next."

"Ladies first!" said Camilla, peeling off her mud-encrusted shin-pads, and giving her brother that superior smile that he knew so well. She's won again, Matthew thought. First bath as usual. It just wasn't worth living.

Monday wasn't as bad as Matthew had expected; it was worse.

"It's the Cup Match on Saturday, Matt," said his mates. "That sister of yours will lose it for us. If she starts hacking away at the opposition, she'll get sent off again and we'll be down to ten men. Or worse still it'll be like last Saturday and she'll give away all those penalties!"

"You've got to do something, Matt. You've got to stop her."

"I wouldn't let my sister play in the team, anyway."

"If you don't stop her, Matt, we'll lose the Cup."

And so they went on. And Matthew knew they were right. But what could he do? He couldn't say anything to her – it would only make her even more determined to play. Coach wouldn't help; he was scared of her too. There was no way she wouldn't be on that pitch on Saturday morning. And to make matters worse, it was their ninth birthday on Saturday. It wasn't going to be a very happy one. Not for him, at any rate.

Matthew worried all day Monday. He fretted all of Tuesday and most of Wednesday. But then on

Wednesday evening he read something rather interesting in the local newspaper.

"LIAM STOKES TO VISIT TOWN BOOK-SHOP" ran the headline. Matthew's heart seemed to stop beating as he read on. The famous footballer was coming to *their* town to sign copies of his new book. On Saturday morning. The same time as the match.

All at once Matthew felt depressed. It was his big chance to meet Liam Stokes and he wouldn't be able to go. On his birthday, too. Life just wasn't fair.

Then, all of a sudden, he saw a glimmer of hope. More than that, it was the Beginnings of a Brainwave. It was a Flash of Inspiration that sent him cartwheeling around the room. All he had to do was to show this to Camilla, and she'd forget all ideas of playing in the match. She was crazy about Liam Stokes. She had posters of him all over her bedroom wall. She slept with a crumpled picture of him under her pillow. If anyone could get him out of this mess with his friends, it was Liam Stokes. This was the Plan of the Century. What would his friends say when they heard?

"Millie," he said. "Look at this!"

Camilla grabbed the newspaper from Matthew's hands.

"What?" she demanded.

Matthew pointed to the front page.

All was silent for a minute. Matthew wondered for an awful moment if this really was the Plan of the Century. Had his hopes been raised for nothing?

But then Camilla gave a scream of delight. She kissed the newspaper a few times and then skipped around the room, clutching it to her like a skinny dancing partner.

This is it! thought Matthew.

"Don't forget it's the Cup Final match on Saturday," he said gingerly.

"Oh, who cares about the stupid match!" said Millie, her eyes shining. "I'm going to see Liam if it's the last thing I do."

Matthew just made it to the door before nearly exploding with relief and triumph. He'd done it! He had found a way to keep Millie out of the game. All his mates would talk to him now, and they might even have a chance to win. And, what's more, Millie would be in a good mood for days.

*   *   *

It was Saturday morning, a brilliant frosty day when spiders' webs glistened in hedges and grass creaked and crackled underfoot. It was the perfect day for a birthday. It was also the perfect day for a football match. There would be no fouls, no penalties – no Camilla.

The twins opened all their presents, and had a special birthday breakfast in bed. Matthew gave Camilla a poster of Liam Stokes. Camilla didn't give him anything, but she was so excited about meeting her hero that Matthew understood. He could hardly wait to get out on the pitch, and he checked his kit and polished his boots three times in readiness. It was his day, and he felt excited and apprehensive all at once.

But when he came downstairs and saw Camilla, he felt that old familiar feeling creep over him again. Smug, thought Matthew. That was the word for her. He began to feel uneasy, as though this birthday might not be so good after all. She smiled at him, that old familiar smile, the one that Meant Something. Something he wouldn't like.

His worst fears were realized when Camilla sauntered up to him in her team kit, her football boots slung over her shoulder.

"What about Liam Stokes?" he faltered.

"What *about* Liam Stokes?" she replied, and smiled knowingly as she pulled up her socks.

Lost again, thought Matthew. On my birthday, too. Just my luck.

On the way to the match, Dazz, Nadim and Danny kept glaring at Matthew accusingly. He knew what they were thinking: why hadn't he done something to keep Millie out of the match? If only they'd known what a close thing it was, he thought. None of them had a sister who played football: trust it to be him.

"Team, before we start," said Coach, "we have to say Happy Birthday to Matthew and Camilla" – here there were a few muttered greetings – "and now, Camilla has an announcement to make, about a special supporter we have with us today."

All eyes turned to Camilla, who beamed round at her team-mates.

"You couldn't get rid of me that easily, little brother!" she said to Matthew. She was twenty minutes older than him, and never let him forget it. She paused dramatically, and then took a deep breath.

"I wrote to Liam Stokes to see if he would come and watch us play, before he does his book-signing. And, guess what – he wrote back! He said it would be much more fun than sitting in a bookshop all day, so he agreed."

The boys all stared at her, open-mouthed. They just could not believe what they were hearing.

"He's out there now! Come on!" said Camilla, doing a few quick star-jumps. "It's nearly time for kick-off!"

Usually, Millie strode on to the field like a Valkyrie in a vicious temper. Like an Amazon looking for an argument. But today, she smiled sweetly at the other team and prettily flicked her pony-tail over her shoulder. Instead of defending like a demon, she played like an angel. You could almost see the halo glowing over her head. While she usually adopted the attacking tactics of Attila the Hun, today she deprived the opposition of the ball without even a tiny kick at their ankles.

When she shook hands with the other captain, they all winced, expecting her to pull him over. But Millie was the essence of politeness. When the opposing number 9 tripped her up, her team-mates couldn't bear to watch. But Millie quietly accepted his apology and carried on with the game. Not a penalty was given against her. The red card stayed in the referee's pocket. No one, least of all Matthew, could believe their eyes.

The score was 2–2, and they had to play extra time. Just occasionally, Matthew saw the glint of battle in Camilla's eye, but she carried on behaving like a perfect lady. She had scored their team's two goals, and Matthew could see she was aiming for a hat-trick. For the first time ever, he began to feel proud of his sister.

But that was nothing to the way he felt when, approaching full-time, he saw Millie in possession of the ball, racing towards an open goal. She had already wrong-footed the goalkeeper, and wasn't offside. Matthew ran up on her left side. "Go for it, Millie!" he yelled.

Then Millie did a surprising thing. Instead of shooting into the goal, she passed the ball deftly to an astonished Matthew, who picked it up and sent it winging into the net with a triumphant kick. "Goal!" shouted Coach.

Dazz flung his arms round Matthew and so did Nadim. Danny thumped him on the back, and Tom slapped his hands. Matthew stretched his shirt over his head and ran up and down the length of the pitch. It was the best day of his life.

"That was your birthday present, little brother," whispered Camilla, as they all gathered into their centre positions again.

"Don't expect anything else, not for the next ten years. It was for Christmas as well," she added, in case he had other ideas.

"Thanks, Millie," Matthew said. He knew how much she would have wanted that hat-trick, especially as Liam Stokes was watching. Perhaps she wasn't so bad after all.

After the Cup was presented to Dazz, Matthew did a lap of honour, lifted high on Liam's shoulders. He had scored the winning goal. But they all decided on the Man of the Match. It just had to be Millie.

JANE BATES

Jane Bates was born in London and now lives in Winchester with her husband, Chris, and her two children – Catherine, fourteen, and Alexander, eleven. Before the arrival of her children she worked as a nurse and a midwife, and now she works in a playgroup and as a childminder. She is fairly new to writing, but has won a few competitions and had several articles published. She's now working on a crime novel. Jane's favourite recreation is watching football – she is a Chelsea supporter.

She says: "As a child I spent hours writing stories and poetry. Over twenty years later I started story-telling again, for my own children, and for the children I work with at the local playgroup; encouraging them to use their own imagination and powers of invention in the same way. Television is unavoidable but is passive entertainment, and children need to be enticed to read by material that is dynamic and visual, with plenty of humour thrown in. That's what I'm aiming for!"

Tulshi and the Banyan Tree

JUDITH WAVELL

Illustrated by

GEORGIEN OVERWATER

To the real Tulshi. May she be happy with her tall husband.

T ulshi had been still so long that the small
fishes were swimming round her feet as
she stood in the brook. Her toes looked
like small, brown roots probing the grey shingle
of the stream bed. Perhaps I am putting out roots
too, she thought. A tiger roared in the forest,
making her jump.

Tulshi scrambled up the bank of the stream
with her basket and hurried to her lord and
husband. She made namaskar to him, pressing
her hands together and bowing her head. She
sang to him in her sweet, clear voice, then knelt
on the ground with her basket of food and
garland of flowers.

She was the only girl she knew who had
married a banyan tree and she was very proud of
him. Even for a banyan tree his size was

impressive. His many great spreading branches had dropped down a thicket of roots that burrowed deep into the earth to support their weight.

The tiger heard her singing. Dinner, he thought. Dinner is ready. Dinner is over there waiting for me. Dinner is singing so that I will know which way to go. What an obliging dinner.

The banyan tree had been dozing in the hot sun, barely aware of her. He liked Tulshi. She was a good wife, no trouble at all really, and she brought him gifts each day. A low growl alerted him. He saw the tiger, his yellow and black stripes bright against the green of the rice fields and his tail swishing in anticipation as he prepared to pounce. The banyan tree knew he had to act quickly.

"Grow!" he commanded his roots. "Grow like the wind. Grow as you have never grown before."

A wall of roots dropped down behind Tulshi encircling the tiger. Tulshi, still singing, didn't notice, but the tiger snarled and lashed hard at the roots with his strong claws. Tulshi sprang to her feet and turned.

"Watch that!" said the banyan tree to the tiger. "I don't like being scratched."

"Well, let me have my dinner then," said the tiger.

"That's not your dinner, that's my wife," said the banyan tree. "You're not going to eat her."

"Why not?" asked the tiger. "She's a poor, bent thing. Her back is crooked. She's a hunchback. The reason the villagers married her to you was that none of the village boys wanted her."

"All I know," said the banyan tree, "is that she has a kind face and a sweet voice and she brings me gifts. What more could I want?"

"They cheated you," said the tiger. "The only way her young sisters could marry was if Tulshi married first. They didn't even give the poor girl a dowry."

"Is that true, Tulshi?"

Tulshi blushed. "Perhaps, lord."

"Do you mind about your humped back, Tulshi?"

"Yes, lord," said Tulshi.

"What would happen if I let this tiger eat you? Would the villagers find me another wife?"

"I don't know, perhaps not."

"I see," said the banyan tree, beginning to rustle his leaves very fiercely. "I think I'm about to be very angry. No one should be treated like that!"

"Oh, I'm sorry," said Tulshi, looking scared. She had never seen an angry tree before.

"Not with you, my wife; with those stupid villagers. I think we need to punish them, don't you?"

"I don't know about that," said Tulshi, who was really quite fond of her parents and young sisters.

The tiger had been exploring his tree cage, prowling around, testing the mat of roots and chewing at the mass of boughs with his huge, white teeth. He stretched up to reach the boughs above, looking for a weak place through which he could escape. He looked very large like that, very large and very strong. Tulshi felt quite scared, for he looked so angry and his tail lashed to and fro like a whip.

"Let me out of here," he said, clawing again at the roots which were like prison bars. "Give me my dinner!"

"I don't think so," said the banyan tree. "You

do seem to be in a fearfully bad temper. I think you'd better stay there until you calm down a bit. You see, I'm a vegetarian and I don't like people eating meat under my branches. Besides, she might scream. I don't like to hear young girls screaming."

"I could kill her first," said the tiger eagerly.

"Absolutely not," said the banyan tree. "She may be a poor, bent thing, but she is my wife."

"Thank you, lord," said Tulshi in a rather small voice. "It's good of you to protect me."

"When are you going to let me go then?" growled the tiger. "It's well past my lunchtime."

"It could be months," said the banyan tree. "I don't want you to eat my Tulshi."

"I'll try not to eat her," said the tiger. "Even though I'm so hungry that I could just die, right now!"

"Trying is not enough," said the banyan tree. "Tulshi, you'd better give him my lunch."

"But what about you?" said Tulshi. "Won't you be hungry?"

"I'll manage," said the banyan tree.

Tulshi picked up the basket and the garland of

flowers and took them to the tiger. He sniffed loudly through the barrier of roots.

"What's in there?" he demanded. "It doesn't smell very nice."

"On the contrary, it smells delicious," said the banyan tree.

"Curry and rice, mangoes and bhugias," said Tulshi. "I prepared it myself."

"Ugh!" said the tiger.

"Remember your manners," said the banyan tree. "Or I'll keep you trapped for ever and ever."

"I'll eat," said the tiger.

The banyan tree moved one of its roots just a little, so that Tulshi could slide the basket through the wall of roots to the tiger, then moved it back again quickly.

"Now I want to see a nice clean plate," said the banyan tree. "Don't leave anything! Tulshi, don't watch him feed. It's not a pretty sight."

The tiger growled, but didn't dare to reply. Instead he pushed his great striped head into the basket, and with his harsh, red tongue he licked open the glossy, ribbed banana leaves which held the food.

He grumbled irritably at the rice. It was far too tasteless. The banyan rustled his leaves in warning. Hastily the tiger ate the bhugias and the slices of mango.

The curry burnt his mouth! He snarled. One of the roots, not quite grown into the ground yet, waved warningly above the tiger's head. To dowse the burning in his mouth the tiger ate the banana leaves and the garland of flowers. Bright petals hung from his jaws. Finally he ate the rush basket. It was stiff and scrunchy and hard pieces of rush jammed between his teeth and scratched his throat.

Dinner should not have sung like that, he thought. If dinner hadn't sung, then he wouldn't be here, trapped in the roots of a tree and eating silly things like curry and flowers and rush baskets instead of fresh, red meat. He decided he would never again try to eat a dinner which sang.

"Will you let me go now?" he asked.

"Not yet," said the banyan tree. "I need to think. I haven't finished with you yet. Besides you didn't say please. Tulshi, would you like your back to be straight?"

"Above all things, lord."

"Suppose I grew one of my roots up your spine?"

"Could you do that? I mean, wouldn't it hurt?"

"Well, it might tickle a little, but I don't expect you'd mind that, would you?"

"Not at all," said Tulshi.

"There's one problem," said the banyan tree. "My roots grow down, not up. Can you balance on your hands?"

"Of course," said Tulshi.

"That's a good root, over there," said the banyan tree. "Do you see the one I mean, Tulshi, the one I'm wiggling? Can you stand on your hands underneath it?"

"Yes, lord," said Tulshi.

Carefully she put her hands on to the ground and stood on them, resting her feet on the bough above. Her sari fell over her head so that she couldn't see but she felt the root wriggle its way inside the waist of her sari, then under her skin towards her head. It was a strange sensation, not painful, but as though her body wanted to sneeze. She could feel her ribs moving, pushing and twisting, then there was a jerk as her shoulders straightened. Her neck had been short and twisted, now she could feel her head moving away from her body, just like a pull-out telescope. Finally there was a sharp noise as the root snapped itself off.

"You can stand up now, Tulshi," said the banyan tree.

"My goodness," said the tiger, surprised. "That really is a good-looking dinner."

"Tiger," said the banyan tree. "You are pushing your luck. The only reason I haven't forgotten about you already is that I need your help to punish the villagers for treating my Tulshi so badly. I could go to see them myself, of course, but I have so many roots that walking any distance is very difficult and I might trip over myself."

"I could gobble up some of their children to punish them," said the tiger eagerly, trying to forget the dreadful meal he had just eaten. "They have some very juicy babies in that village."

"I've already told you that I'm a vegetarian," said the tree. "Eating children is not something I could approve of. I think it would be nicer if they made it up to Tulshi. Would you like some new saris, Tulshi?"

"Very much," said Tulshi. "This one is shabby and the colours have faded. And thank you for your root. I feel so tall, just like a princess."

She stretched up her arms and spun round, slender and supple and straight as a young sapling.

"That's all right," said the banyan tree. "Now, tiger, this is my offer. I'm going to grow a root right round your mouth to keep you to your promise."

"But how will I eat?" asked the tiger, worried.

"I'll have my root back later on," said the banyan tree. "It's only on loan, so to speak. If you behave well and Tulshi gets her dowry I'll take it off again. If not, then, well, that's your problem, isn't it. Tulshi, I've written a message on that shiny leaf by your head. Could you pick it, please, and take it to your father?"

Tulshi reached up and plucked the leaf.

"All right, tiger," said the banyan tree. "You're to go to the village with Tulshi and do exactly what she says. If you don't, you will wear that root round your mouth for ever and a day. Now keep still while I grow a knot."

The banyan tree wove a long, supple root tightly around the tiger's mouth.

"I can't talk pro-per-ly like this," said the tiger between clenched jaws.

"You don't need to," said the tree. "You just need to do some tricks when Tulshi tells you."

"Do tricks?" said the tiger with difficulty. "Tigers don't do tricks."

"Oh yes, they do," said the banyan tree. "At least they do if they want their mouths untied again. Now roll over and wave your legs in the air like a kitten, then you can practise sitting up and begging."

The tiger tried to growl, but couldn't. In the end he did as the banyan tree said.

"Very pretty," said the banyan tree. "Very fetching. That should impress the villagers with Tulshi's powers. Now try standing on your head."

The villagers didn't recognize Tulshi to begin with. Her back was as straight as a young tree and her face, which previously they could hardly see, was so pretty. Her hair had fallen out of its plait and curled luxuriantly, like banyan leaves, down her back. She wore a red flower behind her right ear. She walked into the village with her hand on the tiger's neck. They thought at first that a goddess had come to visit them.

The tiger behaved impeccably. Tulshi commanded him to do all the tricks she could think of. She got bolder and bolder. Finally she made him lie on the ground before her and sat on his head. The tiger was too discouraged to do anything but obey.

Tulshi's father read the letter from her husband, the banyan tree, and apologized.

"I didn't know," he said, "that a banyan tree would notice what his wife wore. We must not insult him by letting his wife be shabby. Of course you shall have some new saris."

He went into his house and took three saris, part of the dowry for his three other daughters, and gave them to Tulshi. They were glorious – one was of peacock blue with gold patterning, one was soft green and a third was a red wedding sari with rich golden embroideries.

"There you are, my daughter," he said. "I

wish you joy." Tulshi made obeisance to her father. Impulsively he put his hand on her head in blessing.

"Thank you, father," she said. "Thank you very much."

"I'm tired," said Tulshi to the tiger, for she was beginning to enjoy her power. "Perhaps I could ride on your back." The tiger would have growled, but he couldn't because of the root. Instead he let Tulshi clamber on him and plodded wearily back to the banyan tree with her.

"Well done," said the banyan tree, when he saw the brightly-coloured saris Tulshi held in her arms. "Have you had a happy day, wife of my heart?"

Tulshi smiled.

"Yes, lord," she said. The tiger tried to growl again, but the root still bound his mouth.

"Tulshi," said the tree. "I think it might be an idea if you climbed high into my branches before I untie the tiger's mouth."

Tulshi obeyed, but she needn't have worried. As soon as the tiger was free he began to run, as fast as he could, away from that banyan tree, and for all I know he's reached the South Pole and is feasting on the penguins.

Sari: *The sort of dress Indian and Bangladeshi girls wear.*
Namaskar: *The traditional Asian greeting. Press your hands together and bow your head.*
Dowry: *The gifts given to the husband of a girl when she marries.*
Mango: *A tropical fruit.*
Bhugia: *A sort of savoury, spicy doughnut.*

There really is a girl called Tulshi. She comes from a village near Barisal Town in the district of Barguna in a country called Bangladesh.
  She married her banyan tree on February 17th, 1994.

Judith Wavell

Judith Wavell lives in Reading, Berkshire. She has three grown-up daughters and a son, as well as a husband who speaks Burmese and Mandarin. She was a nurse and is now a health visitor, working mostly with mothers and children under the age of five. She had a story called "The Basement" published in the London Magazine *last year. She enjoys writing and reading, mountain-walking and exploring strange places.*

She says: "I made up stories for my four children when they were younger, which was fun. This is the first time I have written a children's story down.

"I like writing for children because you need to have bright pictures in your head. Adults aren't so good at pictures. They don't have any in most of their books. Also adults think they know what is real and what is pretend, and they don't laugh as much as children.

"I have written two novels and some stories for adults. The novel I am writing now meant I had to go into the Syrian desert. There we found a huge jagged, red castle on a red, dusty hill. Far away you could see an oasis. Perhaps I shall write one day about what happened in that castle."

Trick or Treat

Evelyn Goldsmith

Illustrated by
Peter Kavanagh

For my family

M att was alone in the blackness. He took a deep breath and flicked on a torch.

A gruesome head hovered inches from his face, its grisly eyes looking straight into his.

He sprang back with a muffled scream and the torch crashed to the ground.

There was a heavy tread outside the room.

"What's going on in there?" The man's voice was raised, sharp with suspicion.

"Nothing," said Matt.

He switched on a light and took another look in the mirror.

It was truly horrible. Huge bloodshot eyeballs bubbled out of the green warty slime of the skin. Eyebrows like poisonous caterpillars fought for space with the mad tangled mass of hair that fell over the forehead and down in front of the ears. Food was trapped between crooked teeth and maggots dangled over the bloated lower lip.

If the mask frightened *him*, what would it do to everyone else?

He kept it on and felt his way downstairs. The eye-holes were a bit small and he couldn't see the steps.

Mum was in the kitchen, her back to the door.

Matt crept up behind her, a growl rising in his throat.

The shrill sound of the doorbell ripped through the silence and Matt jumped, his nerves shredded.

Mum turned, ignoring the horror of the thing behind her. "That'll be Ben, I suppose."

Matt ground his teeth. He should have known his mum was bomb-proof.

He went to the front door, dragging on a coat.

Dad stood at the bottom of the stairs and watched him go. "Be careful, now. Lots of weirdos about tonight. And don't go to the Malkins' place."

Matt mumbled and slammed the door behind him.

In the porch light Ben and Matt sized each other up.

"Couldn't you get a mask then?" asked Ben.

"You're jealous," said Matt. "You look about as scary as Mickey Mouse."

Outside the gate they turned right, away from the centre of the village.

In the open countryside the wind blew from Siberia. Matt shivered and stuffed his hands deep in his pockets.

"Let's try here," said Ben. "Old Mrs Griggs might be good for something."

They went up the crazy path that led to the cottage and knocked boldly.

There was a long wait before a twenty-watt bulb came on in the porch.

A tremulous voice filtered through the door. "Who is it? What do you want?"

Before Matt could stop him Ben said, "Trick or treat."

Idiot, she'd never open the door now.

Matt turned away.

A narrow shaft of light hit the ground as the letterbox opened, and the end of a walking stick jabbed into Matt's leg, sending him flying.

As he scrambled to his feet he saw a pair of malevolent old eyes peering at him through the slot.

"Trick, I think," said Mrs Griggs.

There was a crackling cackle. The letterbox snapped shut and the porch light went off.

"Where now?" asked Ben.

Matt looked round nervously.

The moon cast pale shadows in a ghostly, unreal landscape.

Ben's mask didn't help. A terrifying skull covered his head. It gleamed white in the moonlight and at every step Ben took, the lower jaw opened and shut. Matt found it unnerving, as if the skull was trying to communicate from beyond the grave. And that wasn't all. A small striped snake, horribly real-looking, was threaded in and out of the eye-sockets.

Matt tore his eyes away from the mask and tried to think.

At last he said, "How about the Malkins' place?"

"OK."

They walked in silence for a while.

"You been there before?" asked Ben.

"Yes. My grandpa used to know Gregory Malkin," said Matt. "I went there with him once. He and his brother are scientists. They invent things."

"What sort of things?" asked Ben.

"Oh, I dunno. But Grandpa says they're brilliant."

"We turn up here," said Matt.

The lane was narrow, hemmed in on both sides by shaggy hedges that snagged their jackets. Nettles and brambles grew dank and thick in the hedge bottoms.

"Doesn't look as if they drive up here much," said Ben. His voice sounded too loud, like shouting in church.

"No, I think they use bikes."

The lane went on and on until at last it ended with a five-bar gate.

They climbed the gate and looked around.

"Wow!" said Ben.

A massive square house rose before them, set

in a gently billowing lawn. The pale stone of the house glowed in the moonlight, and windows on the ground floor were lit, casting golden rectangles on to the terrace.

They walked up broad stone steps to the front door and Ben pressed the doorbell. They heard a distant ringing inside the house.

It was freezing. Ben blew into his hands and Matt stamped up and down on the spot as they waited for someone to come.

There was the sound of a bolt being drawn back. The huge door creaked open and a very tall, thin old man with wispy white hair stood there. He looked like an elderly vicar.

He gazed at them over a pair of round, wire-framed glasses.

"Yes?" he said gently, not seeming to notice the masks.

"Trick or treat," said Matt. He tried to sound confident but his voice didn't work properly and it came out as a sort of squeak. He knew who this was. It was Gregory Malkin.

And he'd just remembered why his grandfather didn't come here any more.

*　　*　　*

"I'm sorry?" said Mr Malkin.

"Trick or treat," said Ben.

"Ah yes, I see. Of course, it's Hallowe'en. Do come in, boys. I expect Cook's got some cakes somewhere."

He beckoned them in with a skeletal hand. As they stood waiting in the hall he closed the door and pushed the bolt home.

"This way," he said, leading them through the hall and down a passage.

He really is very tall, thought Matt. And very thin. Like a stick insect. Or – he gulped – a praying mantis. A tatty green cardigan hung from his shoulders, weighed down by bulging pockets, and his skinny corduroy trousers finished about three inches above his shoes, as if he couldn't get anything with long enough legs.

The passage was wide and well lit. Not at all menacing. But fear fluttered in Matt's stomach.

They passed several closed doors, stopping at one near the end of the passage.

Mr Malkin turned and smiled briefly, then opened the door and stood back to let them in.

Matt took off his mask and looked around.

The room was high, but not very big for a house of that size. It seemed to be a kind of study, softly lit and welcoming. The walls were papered in deep red and the floor was of polished wood covered in rich-looking rugs. A cheerful fire burned in the grate and in front of the fire was a comfortable leather sofa.

It was several seconds before Matt noticed they were not alone. A man was seated in the corner of the room, writing at a big roll-top desk.

Matt nudged Ben and muttered, "Take off your head."

The man swivelled his chair and looked at them. Then he rose and limped towards them, hand outstretched.

"Good evening, boys," he said. "I'm Leonard Malkin."

And Matt's blood froze in his veins.

Leonard Malkin was badly deformed, with a humped back and one leg shorter than the other. But worse than that, his face looked like a rotten apple with a pair of pale eyes peering from among the wrinkles like the grubs of a codling moth.

Gregory saw the boys' expressions and said, "I'm sure my brother will not mind if I explain that a careless nursemaid dropped him as a baby and he rolled into the fire."

Matt couldn't think of anything to say. He nodded sympathetically.

For once Ben was quicker off the mark. He took the outstretched hand and said, "Nice to meet you."

"Now then," said Gregory. "I promised cakes. Perhaps you would like to take a seat while I go and see Cook."

Matt and Ben laid their masks on a small table and sank into the sofa. It was blissfully warm and comfortable and their fears receded.

Then Matt noticed that Leonard had not left the room.

Neither had he returned to his desk.

He limped up to them and stood beside the sofa.

"I think you'll be safer," he said softly, "if you're strapped in."

And quick as a flash he pulled a seat-belt across and snapped it into place.

*   *   *

Matt tried to undo the belt but it wouldn't budge.

A crack appeared in the face hovering over them. It seemed to be a smile.

"I'm afraid it's a special catch," said Leonard. "Our own invention," he added proudly, and went to the door.

As he left the room he said over his shoulder, "Don't worry, you'll be quite safe."

As soon as he'd gone the boys tried frantically to wriggle free, but it was hopeless. It was no ordinary seat-belt. They sank back, defeated.

"Did you say your grandfather *knew* these two?" asked Ben.

"Yes. Grandpa and Gregory Malkin were great friends at one time, but he never sees him now."

"Why not?" asked Ben.

"They killed a man."

"What!" Ben looked at him in horror. "What are we doing here, then? Are you crazy?"

"I didn't remember until he opened the door."

"We could still have run, couldn't we?"

"My brain went kind of paralysed," said Matt. "I didn't know what to do. Anyway, they didn't kill him on purpose. He died of a heart attack."

"And what caused this heart attack?" Ben spoke slowly, as if to the village idiot.

"Fright," said Matt.

The lights dimmed.

As they looked at each other in alarm the floor opened and they dropped into darkness.

The drop was so fast their stomachs stayed on the floor above, but they landed gently.

"Where are we?" asked Ben. His voice trembled.

Matt took a deep breath and gripped the arm of the sofa. "Dunno."

"Can you see anything?"

"No." Matt strained his eyes. "Hang on, what's that?"

He could see something pale forming in the darkness some metres away.

"A skeleton," said Ben, laughing. "It's just a ghost train thing."

Matt didn't answer. People didn't die of fright in ghost trains.

The skeleton faded.

Then the sofa began to move forward, slowly and silently as if on a cushion of air.

Suddenly they stopped and a dim light came on above them, illuminating a mirror.

They saw themselves seated in the sofa. But the heads they saw reflected were those of the Malkin brothers.

Matt sat still, rigid with horror. Ben screamed and clawed at his face. The mirror reflected him exactly except that his head was that of a thin old man with wispy white hair and pale blue, watery eyes.

Matt tried touching his own face. It felt like the rotten apple in the mirror, wrinkled and rough. There was a roaring in his ears and the world spun.

Matt came round to the sound of Gregory Malkin's voice.

"I'm sorry if you were alarmed by our experiment," he said.

The boys were still seated in the sofa, but they were back in the study in front of the fire. There was no sign of the seat-belt. A low table held a tray of tea things and a plate of cakes.

Leonard Malkin was pouring tea into delicate china cups.

He handed one to Matt.

"Better now?"

"Er, yes, I think so," said Matt doubtfully. It felt as if his brain had been taken out and put back in the wrong way round.

"Do help yourselves to cakes," said Gregory. He smiled. "That is what you came for after all."

After three cakes and two cups of tea Matt felt a bit better. "You said something about an experiment."

"Yes," said Leonard. "We're very grateful to you. We're doing some research and it's not easy to find exactly the right..."

"Victims," said Matt.

"Well, yes," said Gregory. "I'm afraid that would be the right word."

Leonard nodded. "We designed an experience using a mixture of computer technology and mirrors."

"And you didn't want anybody who was going to have a heart attack," said Matt.

Gregory nodded gravely. "You heard about that. It was tragic. Everyone blamed us, of course, but it wasn't actually our fault. Steven was an old friend of ours. We'd been telling him about some of the work we were doing, and he wanted to take part."

"We strongly advised him against it," said Leonard. "He was not at all suitable. Too old, too vulnerable. But he insisted."

They fell sadly silent.

"How did you know *we* wouldn't have heart attacks?" asked Ben. "Matt almost did."

Gregory smiled. "You chose yourselves. You're young – what are you, twelve?" The boys nodded. "And you're not easily frightened or you wouldn't be prowling round places like this late at night, especially wearing those magnificent masks."

"I can see," said Matt, "that you can do tricks with trapdoors and computers and mirrors and all that stuff. But how did you make my face *feel* like..." He stopped, embarrassed.

"A rotten apple?' suggested Leonard.

Matt nodded. "I don't see how you changed my *skin*."

"We didn't change your skin," said Gregory, laughing. "Our aim was to make your experience so convincing you actually *believed* you had that head on your shoulders." He rubbed his hands together in triumph. "And it worked!"

Half an hour later Matt let himself in the front door.

"That you, Matt?"

He walked into the living room.

His mother was sitting watching television.

She looked up and nodded approvingly. "That's much better. Really horrific. Where did you get it?"

Matt laughed. That old joke.

He stood for a while watching the screen.

Then he turned to leave and caught sight of his reflection in the darkened window.

He stood, frozen with horror. *Leonard Malkin's head was still there!*

A strangled scream forced itself from his throat and his mother leapt up.

"What's the matter? Oh, don't be silly, Matt, it's only Mr Malkin."

She went to the front door.

Matt heard someone speaking in a low voice. Then his mum said, "It's terribly kind of you,

Leonard. My husband did *tell* Matt not to bother you, but you know what boys are."

She came back into the living room carrying Matt's mask. "Isn't he a lovely man? You left this at their place and he came out specially in case you needed it."

EVELYN GOLDSMITH

Evelyn Goldsmith still lives in the house where she was born, in Southwick, West Sussex! She is married to Alan, and they have two grown-up children and five grandchildren. Evelyn is an Honorary Fellow of the Department of Graphic Design at Brighton University, and has had a book published on the subject of Illustration, as well as many children's dictionaries for Collins and OUP. She enjoys painting and gardening.

She says: "In the mid-eighties a contact at Collins commissioned me to write a dictionary for children. In order to establish a realistic headword list I sent questionnaires to more than three hundred schools all over the UK. Among other things I asked them to list the ten favourite books of their eight-year-olds. Books by Roald Dahl easily filled the top six places. I went through each of the books listing content words and from these I selected the headwords. This exercise gave me some insight into children's taste in fiction – confirmed later when three of my grand-daughters became addicted to Point Horror!"

The Big Eat

MALCOLM YORKE

Illustrated by
SUE HEAP

To the children of Atkinson Road
Primary School, Newcastle on Tyne.

In a distant country lived a family called Snook. There was Pappy, Mammy, Grammy (Pappy's Mammy) and young Gwappy Snook all trying to make a living from their little farm. This was difficult because the earth was too hard, the summers too hot, the winters too cold, the springs too wet and the autumns too foggy – so all they could grow was a little corn to make into bread. They also collected grey yukky berries from their thorny yukky bushes and drank cold water from the well in their backyard. They had a scrawny hen called Carmen who laid one egg every month. Mammy Snook boiled this egg and carefully cut it into four helpings as a special treat. Life was mighty tough for the Snooks.

When the evenings were cold, or wet, or foggy,

119

they sat warming their hands over a candle and Grammy told them old stories. These always involved young sons who married princesses, or found treasure, or changed ordinary things into gold by magic, or they were about mysterious strangers who appeared and granted three wishes to people who had been kind to them. They loved these stories and would go off to their plank beds and mattresses stuffed with yukky twigs much cheered up by them.

Now, one blazing summer morning, young Gwappy was out picking yukky berries. Each prickly bush grew only seven or eight berries at a time so it was hard work. After three hours he had only half filled his bucket, but he was so hot he stopped to have his snack of dry corn bread and bottle of well water in the shade of a rock.

Then he noticed a figure slowly approaching across the scorching fields. As the person neared, he realized it was a raggedy old woman hobbling along with two sticks.

Aha, thought Gwappy, this is obviously one of the mysterious strangers Grammy tells us about in her tales. All I've got to do is be kind to her and she'll give me three wishes and I'll live happily ever after.

So he stood up and greeted her politely, "Good day, ma'am, can I help you?"

She replied, "Good day, young man. May I sit with you in the shade for a few minutes?"

"Of course." Gwappy made room for her. "And would you like a drink of water?" That should impress her with how kind I am, he thought.

Thirstily she drank half the water from his bottle, but said nothing. He would obviously have to try harder if he was going to get those magic wishes out of her, so he said, "I've only one piece of corn bread and fourteen yukky berries, but you are welcome to have half of each."

The old woman thanked him and ate them, then she fell asleep in the shade, snoring loudly.

Baffled, Gwappy returned to collecting yukky berries. This stranger was obviously not going to give him his three magic wishes without a lot more persuasion, so he woke her up and said, "I have to go back to the farm now because Mammy needs these berries for the meal. Why don't you come along and share it with us, ma'am?"

"You're very kind, young man. I'll come gladly," she said.

Pappy, Mammy and Grammy Snook recognized immediately what kind of visitor Gwappy had brought back – a magic one – so they made a fuss of the old lady and asked her to sit down and eat with them. "We have very little but we'd be happy to share," said Pappy, bowing and smiling with all his teeth.

After the meal she thanked them, but made no mention of the three wishes they were expecting. So they tried even harder to appear generous and made up a bed for the old lady. When she was snoring Mammy whispered, "Don't worry, she'll give us our wishes over breakfast," and they all went off to bed hugging themselves with greedy glee.

However, when they woke in the morning the old lady had vanished. The Snooks were furious!

"We've been tricked!" bellowed Pappy.

"All that food given away for nothing!" screamed Mammy.

"And she had my blanket!" snarled Grammy.

"And I wasted my breath being polite!" groaned Gwappy and slammed out in a temper. Then he discovered the stranger had pinned a note to the door with a yukky thorn. It said:

YOU SHARED WHAT LITTLE FOOD YOU HAD. NOW YOU WILL NEVER BE HUNGRY AGAIN. WHATEVER FOOD YOU WISH FOR WILL APPEAR. USE THIS GIFT WISELY.

"Phew, I thought for a moment she'd cheated us out of what we deserved," Pappy admitted.

"Still, it's pretty mean only giving us one wish instead of three," Mammy complained.

"Anyway, let's try it," said Gwappy. "I wish for some butter on my bread."

And instantly the dry crust in his hand was spread with yellow butter.

"I wish for some jam on mine," said Mammy.

And there it was, strawberry jam, oozing over her bread.

"I wish for some cheese with mine," said Pappy.

And on his plate there was a wedge of crumbly cheese.

"I wish for some sugar on my yukky-berry porridge," said Grammy.

And there it was, glittering like frost all over her grey porridge.

Well, they ate their breakfasts with gusto and went off to their tasks around the farm.

When Gwappy had a break from gathering yukky berries he said, "I wish I could have an apple," and it appeared in his hand, all juicy red. He added, "and a glass of milk." There it was, creamy and cool.

When the family gathered for the evening meal Mammy said, "I haven't cooked any bread or yukky berries because I've realized we can now wish for our food. What shall we have?"

"I wish for shepherd's pie," said Pappy.

"I wish for rice pudding for afters," said Grammy.

"And I wish for an orange each to finish," said Gwappy.

"And a nice pot of tea," Mammy added.

They had a wonderful meal, the best they'd ever tasted.

Then, as they drank their tea, Pappy suddenly realized: "We never need work on the farm again!"

Yippee! Gwappy needn't collect yukky berries; Pappy needn't grow corn; Mammy needn't bake bread, and Grammy needn't haul water up out of the well. All they had to do was wish!

Over the next few weeks they had a marvellous time wishing for all the foods they could think of. They had potatoes boiled, fried, chipped, mashed and roasted, and eggs every way they could imagine. They tasted bananas, grapes, mangoes, peaches, nectarines, plums, coconuts and raspberries for the first time ever. They had all sorts of good plain bread and cheese and fish and meat and vegetables, and it all tasted wonderful.

Because they no longer worked on the farm the cornfields soon became full of weeds, the yukky bushes went wild, and the berries rotted on the ground. Nobody remembered to feed poor Carmen so she ran away and was never seen again. Even the well began to fall in now that they could drink squash, wine, coffee, lemonade, champagne or beer, just by wishing for it. None of this neglect mattered one little bit now their magic wishes filled their plates.

After some weeks they became bored with ordinary food so Pappy wished for a big salmon and went into the nearby town and swapped it for lots of cookery books. Now they had prawn cocktails, turtle soups, duckling with oranges, barbecued ribs, sweet and sour pork, spaghetti, kebabs, vindaloo curries, strawberry shortcake, chocolate ice-cream, and sherry trifle.

Soon the once scraggy Snooks began getting fatter and fatter. Because they'd no work to do they sat round the table most of the day thinking up new foods to try, until the days passed in one long meal from morning to night. They tried jambalaya, sushi, kugelhupf, enchiladas, moussaka, crab gumbo, borsch and lobster thermidor. When they tired of those they went on to chow mein, gazpacho, truffles, cassoulet and baked Alaska. They tried a new fruit, a new soup, a new meat, a new fish, a new wine, and a new pudding every few hours.

Pretty soon their clothes were popping buttons, splitting seams, and the zips would no longer close.

"We need some more clothes," wheezed Mammy as she toyed with her peacock casserole.

"But we've no money," Pappy pointed out, swigging from his tankard of sherry, then burping.

Grammy pushed away her plum pudding after only one spoonful and said, "No problem. The town folks are still as poor as we used to be, so why not take some food and bargain for some new clothes?"

"Great idea!" said Gwappy, nibbling a pork pie. "I wish for a big box of kippers."

So they went off to town and swapped the fish for new, bigger, clothes. Of course the townspeople were curious to know where the poverty-stricken Snooks had suddenly got such wonderful food, and how they'd got so fat so quickly.

Gwappy boasted, "It's easy: all we have to do is wish for whatever food we like and there it is, more than we can eat."

When the Snooks had waddled off home the townspeople got together and said, "If they've got so much food they can't eat it all, and it's free, why can't they give some to us? We are nearly starving on corn and yukky berries, just like they used to be, so surely they'll understand and be generous to us."

The townsfolk all walked out to the farm and politely asked the Snooks if they could please wish for a little extra food and pass the left-overs on. The Snooks were indignant.

"Push off, you lazy beggars!" said Pappy and reached for his shotgun.

"Away and work for your living!" said Mammy.

"You've never done anything for us so I don't see why we should do anything for you," Grammy said.

And Gwappy added, "The magic wish was obviously given to us because we're special. Now get off our land."

The people went away muttering angrily.

"Huh, some folk don't know what's right and proper," said Grammy, and went back to her venison stewed in brandy.

"The trouble is, they'll be back," Pappy said as he dipped into his clam chowder.

"We'll have to defend ourselves," Mammy decided, banging down her soup spoon.

Gwappy suggested, "Why not get some guard dogs to scare them away?" The others agreed this was a good plan. So they wished for eighty tins of beans and then swapped them for four very fierce dogs they called Slobber, Snarl, Snappy and Yappy.

Now they could safely settle down to eat their scrambled eggs with oysters, candy-floss, guacamole, chocolate fudge, rabbit in pomegranates, blancmanges, frogs' legs and syllabubs.

Occasionally the townspeople came to plead for scraps of food to help them survive the hard winter, but always the fierce dogs and Pappy's gun drove them off.

By spring the Snooks were so fat they had to get a carpenter to widen the doors. They each had several chins and great balloon-like stomachs so they couldn't reach to put their shoes on. When they sat on the furniture it smashed to firewood, and they had to trade some food for steel chairs and beds. As they picked at more and more strange dishes (termites in chocolate, shark soup, elephant fritters, badger risotto, four and twenty blackbirds baked in a pie) they threw what they couldn't eat to the dogs, who also got fat and lazy. Eventually they all – Pappy, Mammy, Grammy, Gwappy,

Slobber, Snarl, Snappy and Yappy Snook – were so bloated they couldn't leave the house.

Exactly one year after she'd left, the old woman returned and knocked at the door. One dog (Slobber) looked up and growled, but then went back to snoring with the other three.

"Whoever you are go away, or I'll shoot you with my gun," Pappy shouted from his steel settee.

"But I'm just a poor old lady who needs a drink of water and a crust of bread," she called through the door.

"Push off and earn your own," Mammy yelled from her iron rocking-chair.

"If we gave you some we'd soon have every hungry beggar in the country snivelling at our door," said Grammy.

"You heard, be off with you!" shouted Gwappy and scooped up another helping of curried chicken with custard.

"Couldn't I have even a few yukky berries?" asked the old lady pitifully.

"Yukky berries!" All the Snooks laughed and laughed. "Only poor people eat yukky berries. Not us!" sneered Pappy.

The old lady turned away from the door and uttered a terrible curse.

After a few minutes Pappy said, "That shouting's made me hungry. I wish for a knickerbocker glory with double mayonnaise, cherries and a dollop of ketchup," and he held out his podgy hand.

Nothing happened.

Mammy said, "I wish for some kangaroo chops cooked in camel's milk, hedgehog crisps and marshmallows."

Nothing happened.

Grammy said, "I wish for pepperoni pizza with vanilla ice-cream on the side and a bottle of sherbet."

Nothing happened.

And then Gwappy said, "I wish for a triple whammyburger with treacle sauce."

When nothing happened again they stared at each other in horror.

They sat for a long time thinking, until finally Mammy struggled out of her steel chair and wobbled over to the window. "I'm hungry. I wonder if Carmen has laid any eggs recently." But she could see from the window that

Carmen's coop was empty.

Pappy puffed over and said, "I'll cut some corn so we can make bread." But he could see that the fields were full of thistles.

"And the yukky bushes have gone wild," wheezed Gwappy, who had joined them.

"And the well's fallen in," wailed Grammy.

"We're worse off then we ever were!" groaned Pappy.

"We'll have to start all over again!" howled Mammy, and the others howled with her.

The Snooks went into town to ask for help, but the townsfolk laughed and said, "You told us to go away and earn our own food. You do the same." However, the Snooks managed to swap the gun and dogs for corn and yukky seeds and they began to work again, though they were so fat it was very hard indeed.

Pappy dug a new well, Mammy and Grammy weeded and planted the cornfields and Gwappy sowed and watered new yukky bushes. They toiled in the heat and slowly the fat began to disappear from their sweating bodies. They ate very little meanwhile because the corn was slow to grow and the yukky berries slow to ripen.

One evening the hungry Snooks sat at their meal of corn bread, yukky berries and cups of well water.

Pappy said, "Well, it's been a hard lesson but I'm sure we've all learned something valuable from this experience."

"That's true, we have indeed," Mammy nodded.

"We'd be real idiots if we hadn't," Grammy admitted.

"It's this," said Gwappy, "the lesson we've learned is NEVER, NEVER, BE KIND TO OLD LADIES!"

And the other three nodded their heads and loudly agreed.

MALCOLM YORKE

Malcolm Yorke was born in Sheffield, and now lives in Newcastle upon Tyne with his wife, Mavis. He has two grown-up children, Rachel and Jonathan, and has taught all his life – at all levels from primary to University Ph.Ds. For the last twenty-eight years he has trained English teachers in Newcastle. His main writing is for adults, mostly biography and art history, but he's also written many books for children, including four books for Scholastic! He likes to walk in the mountains, play tennis, paint and sculpt.

He says: "I read and told stories to my own children, and to all the children I ever taught. When I trained teachers I always insisted they shared stories with their classes and had a go at writing them. Stories are important because they are ways of sharing humour, exploring different times and places, meeting new people, and adding to your store of words and ideas."

The Folding Boy

KATE SCARRATT

Illustrated by
PETER BAILEY

To all the storytellers.

There once was a boy who lived in a house with his parents and grand-parents. In the other houses in the village lived uncles and aunts and neighbours, and children he went to school with. They were all kind, and he grew up in a world full of people who loved him, but he puzzled them. "He's a good boy," they would say, "but somehow ... well, you know, he's not quite like us."

They didn't say this to his face, of course, because they were fond of him, but even so the words somehow made their way to him. He took these words and carefully put them with all the other words he found, and when he was alone he would spend hours arranging them into stories and dreams.

At first he kept all the stories in his head, but

after a time he had so many that he feared they would get muddled and jumbled, and so he looked for a way to keep them safely. He began to collect cast-off scraps of brightly-coloured paper and card, and from these he learned to cut and fold the most beautiful little boxes, decorating them with twists and curls of left-over yarn from his mother's sewing basket, or with little glowing pieces of glass, blue and green and purple; and into each box he put a story, or a dream, or a fantastic animal or shape which he had created.

After a time he became very quick and clever at making all these things and his friends began to envy him his strange talent, although they could see no use whatsoever for it. "What is the point," they said, "of being able to make things out of what other people don't want? In the cold hard world, that won't get you anywhere!" And they laughed at him, to comfort themselves.

His parents and grandparents said the same things. "You're doing well at school, you could grow up to be an important man – a doctor or a lawyer maybe. Why do you waste your time making animals and shapes? And telling stories about them? It's time you grew up!" They started making big plans for him, and took away the paper and card when they found it, to discourage him gently and protect him from being disappointed in life. Then the boy decided to keep things from them so that he could continue telling stories and having dreams.

He passed his exams at school, and the day came when his family and neighbours and friends said to him, "Now you must make up your mind about what you want to do in the world. It is time."

So he told them, "I want to do the thing I do best. I want to go out and tell my tales and make people laugh, and cry, and laugh again."

But everyone scolded him and told him not to be so silly. "Be practical," they said. "These dreams of yours are confusing you – maybe we should take away all those boxes, and then you will settle down."

When he heard this, the boy knew what he had to do. That night when everyone was asleep, he took a sheet of golden card from his store of bits and pieces and swiftly fashioned a tiny new box, the most beautiful he had ever made. It had smoothly curving edges which came together in a point at the top, and was studded with fragments of wine-red and jaybird-blue glass; they caught the moonlight like jewels. Next he took silver card and made another box, every bit as beautiful as the first one. Then he made another and another, and another, until he was working so fast that the little boxes dropped from his fingers like shoals of glittering fish tumbling from a net.

When he had finished, he gathered the boxes and crept up to the room where his grandmother and grandfather lay sleeping. He stood next to his grandfather and very gently began to fold him, placing his arms across his chest and pulling his knees up to his chin; and all the while his grandfather slept peacefully. Smaller and smaller he folded the old man, until at last he could slip him into the golden box. Then he carefully folded his grandmother in the same way, smaller and smaller, until he could place her in the silver box. He went next into his parents' room, and after that into the houses where his cousins lived, folding and storing all the time. Then he went to the neighbours' houses, until by sunrise everyone he knew was safely packed away in a beautiful little box. Then the boy gathered up the boxes and set off towards the world.

When he came to the world he stopped and began to fashion a strange new animal, and soon a crowd of people gathered around him to watch. As he made the animal he told a story about it, and the people laughed and clapped and went away amazed, saying how they had never seen or heard of such a thing before, but now they had seen it they would surely know it again.

The boy continued on his way until he came to a town. There he took out the golden box, the one with his grandfather in it, and unfolded him and began to tell a story about the beautiful objects which the old man, who was a carver, could make. Soon a small crowd, and then a big one, gathered around him to listen to the story, and marvel at the skill of the grandfather and the life he led. As the boy spoke, they could see before them all the chisels and shaving hooks and tiny implements for piercing and chasing delicate details into the wood. When the boy had finished, he folded up his grandfather and the people went away saying what a clever boy he was, and how true his tale.

The boy grew to be a man, spending his life wandering through the world folding and unfolding his dreams and stories. He built himself a house, but spent little time in it. Everything he had, he kept in a box which he made specially; and everything he had, he used in a story. Sometimes people were almost afraid to talk to him, in case he folded them up and used them in his stories too, but although he often did, they never realized what he had done.

Doctors and lawyers and engineers would come to relax and listen to his tales at the end of each day. Sometimes they said to him, "Oh, but you have an easy life, just telling stories all the time! You should do my job, a proper day's work, then you'd see what a hard place the world really is."

The man only smiled, and said, "Tell me then, tell me about the world."

The lawyers declared it was a matter of applying the law correctly; everything followed from that. The doctors maintained it was a matter of healing the sick. Engineers wanted stronger bridges and straighter roads, teachers longed for their pupils to listen to them and pay attention. That, they all told him, was what the world was about.

One day the man did not come any more to the towns and villages, and a rumour spread amongst the people that he was dead. But although they looked everywhere, they could find nothing but the boxes he had left behind: there was no trace of the man himself. "Perhaps he has been taken up into heaven," they said to each other, "and is among the saints." But they did not really think so, because after all he had done nothing with his life except tell stories.

As time went by they began to miss him. "It is hard to explain," they admitted, "but something is lacking. We teach and build and heal, but our lives somehow seem empty now the man has gone."

"If we could only find a body," said the doctors.

"Let us go back over the facts of the case," said the policemen and lawyers.

So they made another search, but still all they

could find were the beautiful tiny jewelled boxes which filled every room in the man's house. "Perhaps if we open these," said the people at last, "they will tell us something." So they gathered round and started to open the boxes one by one, hoping to discover what had become of the man.

As each box was opened a story or a fabulous animal or a strange shape would come out, and someone in the crowd would say, "I remember this!" and would start to tell the story as he remembered it; and the new tale would be taken up by other voices, until the whole evening was spent telling and retelling one story. Once again the people discovered the grandfather and grandmother, the cousins and neighbours and strange animals, greeting each one with delight as they unfolded it.

This continue for many many days and nights, until finally, after a very long time, they came to the last box of all; a wonderful box of gold and silver leaf, covered with rubies and emeralds and diamonds and pictures of unknown birds and trees and plants: and on every place that was not decorated with pictures and jewels, there were

words and letters inscribed in a thousand different languages.

"What can be in this one," they said, "but the man we seek? He must have folded himself up and put himself in here!" And so, although fearing greatly to disturb the man inside, they opened this final box too.

"What is in it?" asked the crowd, as the lid was lifted. Out from the box came something folded very small. "Let us see!" they cried, as the shape inside the box was opened out. "What is it? Is it the man?" But it was not the man. Then out from the beautiful box came another shape, and another, and another, and another, until at last the box was empty and every shape had been unfolded and laid out on the ground before the wondering crowd.

Then they stared in astonishment, because they could see quite clearly that what they had found in the box was not the man at all, but themselves, each and every one of them. And the doctors and lawyers, and butchers and teachers and dustmen, exclaimed in amazement. "Were we in the box all the time?" they said, "and not, as we thought we were, out in the world?"

They stood in bewilderment for a long while, not knowing what to do. Then slowly first one and then another came forward from the crowd to claim his own shape, and take it away with him, and listen to the stories it had to tell him. And at long last when all the people had gone, the beautiful box quietly unfolded itself too, and went away, to start again in a new place.

KATE SCARRATT

Kate Scarratt was born in Egypt, grew up in Essex, and now lives in Barry, in the Vale of Glamorgan, with Harvey, her husband. She has taught English to foreign language students and to foreign language teachers, and now works part-time as a co-ordinator of a volunteer bureau in the Vale of Glamorgan. Kate is a member of the Cardiff Astronomical Society with a passionate interest in Shakespeare. She gives talks and short courses on Shakespeare's Theatre to adult education classes in Glamorgan. She has had several poems and stories published, but this is her first piece of children's fiction.

She says: "The best stories for children – good strong stories, well-observed, which tell the truth and never talk down to the reader – can be enjoyed by any age group.

"Unfortunately most people won't get to know much about the 8,000 titles published this year. There's virtually no major media interest – the Independent *being an honourable exception. Add to this a decline in library services generally, and where do parents and teachers go for information and informed advice? Children's literature is proper literature, and the stuff our earliest dreams are made of. We should all demand a higher profile for it."*

The Joke

SARA CARROLL

Illustrated by
KATE SHEPPARD

For my parents

Andrew Picklefinger had two passions in his life: telling jokes and playing football. He was very good at one of them and very bad at the other, but he loved them equally.

When Andrew started a sentence with the words, "Here's a good one..." people groaned. They walked away with their fingers in their ears, asked him if he'd take a note to the headmaster, or just turned the telly up. It wasn't that he couldn't tell jokes, he just didn't know any good ones. Even if they were new and hilarious to Andrew, other people had always heard them before. They knew why cows wear bells (because their horns don't work) and what goes zub zub zub (a bee flying backwards).

Andrew's bad jokes were famous at West Wind First School:

"Come on, Pickleface, tell us a new one."

"Give up, Picky. We've heard them all."

"Get a new joke book, Picklewiggle."

"One day," said Andrew. "One day I'll tell a joke so funny you'll ... you'll..."

But no one stayed to hear the rest of the sentence. No one expected such a day to arrive.

On the football pitch, things were a lot brighter. Andrew was the greatest goalkeeper the school had ever had. He saved everything – penalties, headers, searing left-footers and fluky deflections from dodgy defenders. Well, everything except the hundred-mile-an-hour rockets from West Wind's answer to Ryan Giggs. Belinda Springs was as skilful at putting balls into the net as Andrew was at keeping them out. In fact, she was better. However hard he tried, however knee-grazing his dives, Andrew Picklefinger had never saved a shot from Belinda Springs and he hated her for it.

There was a lot to like about Belinda – she was at his school for a start (which meant West Wind First Football Team were unbeaten for two seasons) and she always turned up for lunchtime knockabouts. But as far as Andrew was concerned she was better than him, so he couldn't like her.

Andrew followed his grandad round the kitchen with a stream of questions.

"Why did the tap dancer have to retire?"

"Why are cooks bullies?"

"What do you give a sick pig?"

(She kept falling in the sink.)

(Because they beat the eggs and whip the cream.)

(Oinkment, of course.)

"Not now, darling," said his mum. "Why don't you go and play outside?"

Not now, darling. What about your seven times table, love? Could you go to the bottom of the garden and get me something I don't need, sweetheart? It got a bit wearing, the way people constantly found ways of stopping him from telling jokes. Andrew kicked a stone hard against the wall. It had not been a good day. Belinda had got three past him at lunchtime and then he'd been told to tidy the book corner after asking his teacher, Mr Dean, how he could get four elephants into a mini. (Two in the front and two in the back.)

"Andrew!" Grandad was waving something at him from the back door. "Your mother's waiting in the car, and look, I picked this up at a jumble sale on Saturday."

Grandad gave him a book. The picture on the front was of a cat with a huge stomach shaped like a beak on one side. (Because when a cat swallows a duck you get a duck-filled fatty-puss.) The title of the book was *One Hundred Best Jokes Ever*.

"Maybe you'll find a good one in there."

"Thanks, Grandad."

Andrew read the book all the way home. Eventually he plucked up courage and tried one on his mum. As she turned off the engine he gave her the punchline.

"She kept running away from the ball."

He watched her mouth turn up. He could see her teeth as she started to smile, her shoulders began to shake and she turned to him, actually laughing.

"You know, Andrew, that's rather good."

THE JOKE

Andrew couldn't believe it. He'd just told his first funny joke. He'd just told a joke so funny that his mother had laughed, shoulders and all. He told the joke to his brother Angus and he laughed. He told the joke to his dad and he laughed. He even told the joke to the cat and although he didn't laugh, he didn't walk away. This was obviously a really classy joke and he would tell it in school the next day.

The moment for telling a joke has to be chosen with care. There is a split second when it will work; the moment afterwards would be disastrous. Andrew seemed to encounter these split seconds all morning, but he bottled out every time, usually because the very thought of the joke made him giggle, and as every comedian knows, giggling before the punchline will guarantee total joke-failure.

Andrew went out to play football at lunchtime in a bad mood. And his mood got worse. Several of the other team had detention and couldn't play, but Belinda was playing for them (Belinda Springs never had detention) and Andrew's side struggled. He watched Belinda from his goal. She really was good – she ran fast, passed cleanly and never gave up. He saw her start running with the ball, her eye on the net, her mind already set on celebration. OK, thought Andrew, this time. He crouched in concentration, never taking his eye off the ball. Here it came, nearer and nearer. Belinda's red plaits were a blur in the background, her white trainers just a flash. The ball was the thing. He saw her line it up, he watched her swing her leg.

Thud... Splat... Ow!

Andrew had stopped the ball and saved the goal, but he'd saved it with his head and was now lying flat on his back watching the sky dip and swerve towards him.

"Great save, Picklewiggle!"

"You're going to have a mega-bruise on there, Picky."

"Are you all right, Andrew?"

He sat up and felt his forehead. A bruise was rising under his hand. Urgh! And the inside of his head didn't feel much better than the outside. In fact, he felt a bit sick. He stood up, very wobbly.

"I sit think I'd down better," he said, and the others watched him walk off.

Andrew carried on watching the game from a bench and just as he was beginning to wonder if he could still remember his own phone number, he realized what had happened. He had saved a shot from Belinda Springs. He had actually stopped a Springs stinger. He was now her footballing equal and that was worth any number of bumps on the head.

While he was doing his history project, Andrew realized something else that had happened. He'd lost his joke. He could remember the punchline, but where oh where was the question? It must be there somewhere. "Why did the chicken...?" No. "What did the policeman...?" No. He could only find the tired old jokes that he knew and loved, and everyone else knew and hated. All afternoon he kept muttering the punchline to himself.

"Andrew Picklefinger, stop talking and get on with your Viking housework, page thirty-six."

Andrew pretended to read but was really concentrating hard on the joke. But the joke wouldn't come. And to add insult to injury, or rather injury to injury, his head was beginning to throb with pain. At afternoon break Andrew chose not to play football for the first time in the three years he'd been at school. He went to sit in the cloakroom, resting his head in his hands. It was all *her* fault... If she hadn't been so good... If he hadn't wanted to prove he was better... If she hadn't even come to his school. He could feel a clenchy feeling at the back of his throat.

"I mustn't cry. I mustn't cry." But he ran to a toilet and locked the door, just in case.

By the time the bell went for the end of school, Andrew was beginning to feel better. After all, his mother was picking him up and he'd only told her the joke yesterday, she was bound to remember the question. Besides, his head was hurting less, which was some consolation.

He raced out to his mum. "She kept running away from the ball," he said. "What was the question?"

"What? Andrew, what have you done to your head?" He told her about the game and the joke and she was very pleased, then very concerned, but after testing him on his seven times table and asking him to spell marmalade she decided that the joke part of his brain was the only bit that was affected. Andrew was beside himself with frustration.

"Yes, but Mum, what was the question? How did that joke go? Don't you remember, you laughed?"

"Oh, yes... Let me see, it was very funny. Oh, now ... well, darling you've still got the book at home, you can check when we're back."

Home was a hundred miles away, the traffic lights took six days to change and Mum drove in slow motion. Eventually they were home and he raced upstairs to find The Book. But it wasn't under the bed where he thought it would be. It wasn't on the shelf; it wasn't in the wardrobe; it wasn't in his sock drawer, his shirts drawer or his jumper drawer; it wasn't even in that drawer at the bottom which he couldn't shut. He turned his room upside down and inside out, he searched his parents' room, Angus's room and even the bathroom (including the dirty washing basket) but the book of *One Hundred Best Jokes Ever* was nowhere to be seen. He didn't want one hundred jokes, he only wanted one, *that* one, the one that stupid girl had knocked out of his head.

He kept quiet about the fact that he'd lost the book – his mother would think the bump on his head was serious after all – so he couldn't ask Dad or Angus, in case she got suspicious. It was a quiet Andrew Picklefinger that went down to tea. He didn't take his ball into the garden afterwards, he didn't even watch telly. He just sat on his bed looking around the mess in his room, staring into every pile, trying desperately to remember what he'd done with the precious book.

The next day he woke up in a bad mood. He decided to forget about trying to remember where the book was and challenge all his mental powers into remembering the joke itself. But days passed and no joke came, just the pointless punchline over and over again, and Andrew got more and more miserable. He sat at the back of the class, missed lunch, refused to play football and stopped telling jokes. Mr Dean found his quietness so disturbing that he thought he must be ill and dropped him from the match on Saturday. He was long-faced and grumpy when he sat on the wall to wait for his mum to pick him up on Friday.

"Hallo, Andrew!"

Oh no, it was her. Belinda Springs sat down on the wall next to him. They were the last children left. He tried to smile but it came out as a sort of yuk face.

"How's your head?"

"Mmfph!"

"It must be bad for you to miss so much football."

"Urghumf!"

"I'm very sorry ... about the kick ... but you did save it very well."

Andrew began to melt.

"Oh, umfph, thank you."

"And I expect you'll be back in the team next week. I hope so. Peter Herbert is nowhere near as good as you in goal."

Andrew began to melt a bit more.

"You're the best goalkeeper I've ever seen. Better even than David Seaman, I reckon."

Andrew melted a lot.

"Oh ... well ... you're a pretty good striker... Belinda Giggs I call you."

"Oh, thank you!"

There was silence.

"Your mum's late," said Andrew.

"My dad. He's always late. In fact, I think he's forgotten me again."

"Oh, dear."

"We're supposed to visit my granny after school as well, so she'll be worried."

"We're going to see my grandad," said Andrew. Golly, she was just like him. Andrew's mum arrived and he jumped off the wall in relief.

"Good luck for the match."

"Thank you. Bye."

He opened the door and his mother lurched over. "Sorry I'm late, darling. Look, who's the little girl? I can't leave her standing on her own. Does she want a lift?"

Andrew went back miserably.

"My mum says do you want a lift?"

"Perhaps she could drop me at Granny's and I can ring Dad at work. Thanks."

Belinda slid into the back seat next to him. Wow! This was weird. To be sitting next to the person you loathed and hated most in the whole world *and* in your own car. Although she had just been quite nice to him.

She was about to become even nicer.

"Andrew, is this yours?" She was holding up a book with a strange duck-shaped cat on the front.

"BELINDA! YOU'RE BRILLIANT!"

For once, Andrew was pleased to walk into school on Monday morning. The day had come. The day when he could tell a funny joke. As he went into the classroom, Belinda caught up with him.

"We lost. Two–nil. Peter Herbert was useless. We can't wait until you're back. Oh, and good luck with you know what."

As if they knew, the whole class and Mr Dean were waiting for him. He walked through the door and stood next to the teacher's desk. Before Mr Dean could speak, Andrew said:

"I've got something to ask you." He took a deep breath. "Why was Cinderella sent off during the football match?"

Silence.

"She kept running away from the ball."

One by one the class looked at each other and one by one their eyes wrinkled up and they started to smile. Their shoulders shook, they threw their heads back and every single member of 2H laughed loudly.

Mr Dean shook Andrew's hand and his classmates patted him on the back.

Andrew's joke was a triumph. As he made his way to his desk he caught sight of Belinda's face at the window. She winked at him and gave him the big thumbs up.

SARA CARROLL

Sara Carroll was born in Kent and now lives in London with her husband Tim and her eighteen-month-old son, James. She has worked around books and publishing all her life – firstly in a bookshop, then for the Society of Friends (Quakers) in their publications department, and now as a commissioning editor at children's book publishers, Walker Books. Next year, she will have a children's story published, by Walker, under the name of Molly Williams! Before James' arrival she enjoyed watching and performing ballet, but now does more reading, gardening and playing.

She says: "I think I have always wanted to write something, but never believed I would actually get round to it! Since having a baby I have become fascinated with how even tiny babies respond to books – not just the illustrations but also the physical attributes – page turning must be an early instinct.

"However, I have always felt at ease with five to ten-year olds and remember that part of my own childhood with great warmth. I'm not sure I speak for my family there; although I never played football, I did tell bad jokes."

A Long Way to
Cherry Time

DAN JONES

Illustrated by
VALERIA PETRONE

*This story is dedicated to Abram Serfaty,
Ali Bourequat and his brothers, to Ali Idrissi
Kaitouni, Mohammed Nidrani, Jamal Benomar,
Abdellatif Laâbi and to all the hundreds of other
Moroccan and Sahrawi prisoners of conscience
and victims of "disappearance" who were
imprisoned for years for their ideas in Kenitra,
Le Complex, Agdz, Dar al-Mokri, Derb Moulay
Cherif, Tazmamert, Ghbila, Ain Borja,
Layoune, Qal'at M'gouna and secret detention
centres without name.*

TO: *Uncle Latif, 2134 Egypt Road.*
FROM: *Djamila, 24 Zankat Medina.*
Dear Uncle Latif,
So where are you?
We haven't seen you for ages and ages.
No letter either.
Are you ill?
Are you too busy to visit your niece?
Have you gone away?
We all miss you.
Don't forget it's my BIRTHDAY on the 28th.
Mum is making me a dress and trousers.
You must come to my party.
Please write, at once!
Love,
Djamila.
PS And you promised me one of your poems.

TO: *Uncle Latif, 2134 Egypt Road.*
FROM: *Djamila, 24 Zankat Medina.*
Dear Uncle Latif,
So why didn't you come?
Are you upset with us?
You could at least have written.
You always write.
Have you got "Writer's Block"?
Remember our address: 24 Zankat Medina.
We haven't moved.
So I'll be waiting for the postman.
Your affectionate niece,
Djamila
PS DON'T FORGET MY BIRTHDAY.
PPS Mum says she is going to make a cake, mint tea, almonds and *sfinj* – your favourites.

TO: *Uncle Latif, 2134 Egypt Road.*
FROM: *Djamila Habiba, 24 Zankat Medina.*
Oh, my poor uncle,
Cousin Abdelrazzak went to your flat.
Your door was smashed in. He found broken

glass, plant pots tipped over, drawers, books and papers all over the floor.

The old lady downstairs said that Army men had come with guns.

They bumped you down the stairs.

They were shouting.

She said they took your notebooks. She said they threw a blanket over your head, and pushed you into a truck with black windows and no numbers, and drove you away.

Then Mum started to cry.

We are all so worried.

What happened, Uncle?

Was it the Police?

Where are you?

Are you safe?

I don't know if you'll get this letter, but I'm sending it anyway.

A big hug from your Djamila and all at 24.

PS Please come to my party. It's on Friday next week.

TO: *Djamila Habiba, 24 Zankat Medina.*
FROM: *Marcel Lemec, 361 rue Albert, PARIS 9e, France.*

Dear Miss,

You don't know me. But I know you.

This letter is from France. Look at the stamp.

I bring word from Latif the poet, your uncle.

How has this French guy met Latif?

Latif's gone missing, vanished, nobody's seen him.

Well I'VE seen him, dearie.

Me, Marcel Lemec, the pickpocket.

Latif and me, see, we was locked up together in The Complex, underneath the Central Police Station, in chains, in the dark, lying on the stone floor like beasts.

A terrible place.

Intelligence drags poor Latif out each day. He's done nothing. They hurt him, the brutes, to try and make him blab. But Latif won't talk. He says not a word. And when they bring him back, more dead than alive, we whispers together in the cell. He tells me all about your ma and pa, and your birthday.

He must send this letter, he says.

"Madness," I says, because we had nothing, no

card, no pencil, no stamp, no way. Only the old clothes we stands up in.

The brutes said nobody knew we were there. The Complex didn't exist. Intelligence didn't exist. And we didn't exist either, Djamila. We were vanished from the world like a bad dream.

Well one day the brutes say I am to be deported to France.

Your uncle gets excited. He finds a scrap of dry soap.

"Marcel shall be my postman," says he, "and his trousers my notepaper."

He pulls off my jeans, and he scribbles away with the soap on the inside of my trousers. "Walk these words out of the jail, dear trousers," he says. "In France, the pickpocket postman will copy them out for Djamila."

Well those brutes searched me, but they found nothing. So here's Latif's letter, my little jewel. I've copied it as best I could.

My dear Djamila,
I missed your party.
I am so sorry.

Now you are a year older than you were
yesterday. Do you feel different?
In this stinking pit I think of Zankat
Medina, of blue skies, butterflies, cherries
and children laughing. It's very bad in here.
But this will get better. And Postman
Marcel's trousers will carry your birthday
poem.

> It's still a long way to cherry time
> And to hands filled with immediate
>   presents
> The open sky greeting the first morning of
>   freedoms
> The joy of talking
> And the happy sadness

Kiss Ma and Pa for me,
Your fond uncle
Latif

TO: *The Director, Intelligence, DST, Central Police Station.*
FROM: *Djamila Habiba, 24 Zankat Medina.*
Sir,
Please give this letter to my uncle, Abdellatif.
He is a poet.
You will find him in The Complex.
It's the place under your Police Station.
We know he's there.
You know he's there.
And please stop them hurting him.
Thank you,
Yours faithfully,
Djamila Habiba

Dear Uncle Latif,
Will you ever get this letter, I wonder?
"The happy sadness" walked out on
Marcel's trousers.
What a lovely poem! Is there more?
Mum pinned it on the wall in the kitchen.
We cried.
Dad said, "Phew. Latif's alive."
Granny says I grew five centimetres yesterday.
Uncle Latif, I've been digging up our yard to

make a garden.
Dad gave me seeds for my birthday, packs
of alyssum, nasturtiums, petunia, poppies,
zinnia, carrots and artichokes.
I am planting them.
What is your opinion on horticulture?
Love from Djamila, and all at 24 Zankat
Medina.
Kiss kiss kiss

TO: *Djamila Habiba, 24 Zankat Medina.*
FROM: *DST, City Police HQ.*
Unknown at this address.
Return to sender.

TO: *Djamila Habiba, 24 Zankat Medina.*
FROM: *Doctor Ahmed Khaitouni, MD, MRCS,*
Out Patients Department, City Hospital.
Mademoiselle Djamila,

(Forgive me for addressing you in such familiar terms when we have not been properly introduced.)

I work at the City Hospital.

Last night I walked past the Police Headquarters with Fifi.

Something moved above my head. I looked up.

I saw an arm, waving. An arm in chains. Some poor devil, waving.

A small brown package flew in a curved arc over my head.

It bounced on the pavement by my feet and then rolled into the road.

Fifi barked, and ran to pick it up.

It was a Camel cigarette packet, wrapped round a pebble.

Somebody had written "LOOK INSIDE" on top of the camel.

I did and I found this tiny note.

Excuse my reading it.

I send it on to you with the greatest respect, and a bag of dates.

Perhaps I can be of some medical assistance to your uncle?

With kindest regards,

Doctor Khaitouni MD MRCS (surgeon and postman) + Fifi.

Hello stranger! Please help me.
Kindly direct this Camel to:
Miss Djamila Habiba,
24 Zankat Medina.
With many thanks,
Abdellatif,
(poet)

So Djamila,
Did Marcel's trousers walk and talk?
And will this Camel find its way home?
Are you well? And Ma and Pa, too?
Your health is a treasure, Djamila. Have
your new teeth come through?

Your fat Uncle Latif has become your thin
uncle.
Latif's poems have upset a king.
Intelligence pulled out Latif's teeth, but no
new ones will take their place.
There was electricity and water.
Latif's wrists and shoulders hurt where they
hung him up to dry.

The soles of his feet ache from beating. It
hurts him to stand up.
Latif gets headaches, and coughs blood.
They have put him in the Hospital Wing for
repairs.
Ready for some more Intelligence.
But see, Latif has become rich – a stolen
scrap of paper, an empty Camel fag packet,
a broken pen – a king's treasure for the
writer of verses.

More of your poem:
*It's still a long way to cherry time
and to cities filled with wonderful silence
to greet the delicate morning of our loves
the pain of meetings
mad dreams turned into daily chores*
Now I will make this paper jet fly out of the
window to you like a rocket.
All my love
Uncle Latif

TO: *The Director, Intelligence, DST, Central Police Station.*
FROM: *Djamila Habiba, 24 Zankat Medina.*
OK, monsieur,
We all know Uncle Latif is in there.
Look in the Hospital Wing. He's the thin one by the window with bad shoulders and sore feet.
He can't stand up. He needs medicine.
Please let Dr Khaitouni see him immediately.
And please give Uncle this letter, this time. It will make him feel better.
Yours faithfully,
Djamila Habiba

TO: *Djamila Habiba, 24 Zankat Medina.*
FROM: *DST, City Police HQ.*
Unknown at this address.
Return to sender.

TO: *Djamila Habiba, 24 Zankat Medina.*
FROM: *Abu al-Hassan LLD, City Chambers, 52 rue Hims.*
Dear Mademoiselle Habiba,
A letter arrived by air.
I was visiting the Provincial Jail to see a client. A little paper dart glided slowly down the corridor. Where it came from, I don't know. Then it circled slowly round like a white butterfly. I caught it and put it quickly into my briefcase. (I could never make darts.)
It seems to be a letter for you.
Is the writer really Mr Abdellatif Laâbi, the poet? How I admired his brave writing. But it put His Majesty the King into a rage, and he took it out of every bookshop and library.
Your uncle needs a lawyer. Can I help?
With best wishes,
Maître Abu al-Hassan,
lawyer turned postman.

TO: *Djamila Habiba, 24 Zankat Medina.*
FROM: *Prisoner number 3823, Cell 379, Provincial Jail.*
Djamila, my sunshine,

Your nice friend the Doctor Postman came
to see me! Amazing!
He made a big fuss of me and complained
about how the brutes had hurt me. He gave
me medicine. He told me you are growing a
garden.

Now I have been taken out of the black
pit of the Intelligence to a proper jail.
They feed me here, let me wash and shave
and do not beat me. And I'm feeling
better.

I am not alone. I share my little cell with
some small creatures, a lizard and a spider
who eat the mosquitoes, and two
cockroaches with long feelers who eat my
breadcrumbs.
Through the iron bars I can see blue sky and
swallows flying, and people down below.

We aren't allowed to have any visitors or
letters, or books yet. So it's good that I have
managed to keep my secret pen – a broken
Bic biro. (I have chewed off everything

except for the writing end, which I can hide from the guards buried in my curly hair.)
See how prison life has turned Latif the poet into Latif the thief!
One of my poems upset His Majesty, so I am to be charged with:

    insulting kings
    inciting riots
    disturbing public tranquillity

My trial comes up soon. I need a lawyer.
Please see what your dad can do.
I dream of books, flowers and cherries.
A kiss for everybody,
Uncle Latif

TO: *Prisoner number 3823, Cell 379, Provincial Jail.*
FROM: *Djamila Habiba.*
Dear Uncle,
Your paper dart flew all the way to Zankat Medina, and into our front door!
We are pleased you are out of the black pit of hell.

Our latest postman is Maître al-Hassan.
He loves your poems.

Remember you told me to save the pips from those sweet black cherries last summer? I put lots of the pips in the geranium pot.
Well Uncle, you'll never guess!!!
I looked at them yesterday.
Two of the shells have split open. I can see little white shoots coming out.
Baby cherry trees growing up. I have planted them in my new garden.
I water the garden every morning before school.
And Dad's seeds have sprouted. Everything's growing like mad. The carrot leaves are like green feathers. But Cousin Abdelrazzak says it's mostly weeds.
He gave me some tomato cuttings. They have grown up to my knees.
But the cat has scratched up the alyssum, and has peed on the artichokes.
Maître al-Hassan has two small pots for you in his briefcase.
Look after them and you will soon have tomatoes and cherries.

Much love from Dad and Mum, Djamila and the bad cat.

TO: *Djamila Habiba, 24 Zankat Medina.*
FROM: *Prisoner number 3823, Cell 379, Provincial Jail.*
My dearest Djamila,
What a week! Latif Nobody has become Mr Abdellatif Somebody.
On Monday lawyer Maître al-Hassan said he will defend me.
On Tuesday a famous poet phoned the Prison Governor.
On Wednesday they said I can have letters and books.
On Thursday they said I can have visitors.
On Friday an Italian lady came from Amnesty International to campaign for my freedom.
On Saturday they gave me 273 letters that have been sent to me from all over the world.
On Sunday there was a yellow flower on your tomato plant.

Next Friday, dear Djamila, is MY BIRTHDAY.
Please come and see me. Bring your mum and
dad, and some *sfinj*.

> *It's still a long way to cherry time*
> *but already I can feel it*
> *it trembles and rises*
> *sprouting in the heat*
> *of my love for things to come*

Kiss Kiss Kiss
Your fond uncle
Latif

*(The poem is a translation of verses written in Kenitra
jail, Rabat, Morocco by Abdellatif Laâbi, poet and
prisoner of conscience 1972–1980)*

DAN JONES

Dan Jones lives in London with his wife Denise. He has three grown-up children. He has been a teacher and a Youth and Community worker, but has worked for the past years as an Education and Development Officer for Amnesty International UK. He likes drawing, painting, travelling, gardening, and local history. This story is his first published children's work, but he has illustrated many children's books: fiction, educational, and poetry titles. He has also written on human rights issues.

He says: "This book was sparked off by prison letters by the Italian Marxist Antonio Gramsci to his young son about how elephants stand on one leg, and to his sister-in-law about tomato cultivation problems in jail, and by conversations with Moroccan prisoners of conscience and victims of 'disappearance' I have met through my work in Amnesty International.

"As a storyteller I find children from seven to eleven a special audience as readers and listeners, whose gifts of imagination and human empathy are a delight and a challenge."

The children from these schools helped judge
this year's competition:

Chalgrove Primary School, Oxford

Radcliffe on Trent Infant School, Radcliffe on Trent

Radcliffe on Trent Junior School, Radcliffe on Trent

Minehead First School, Somerset

Broke Hall County Primary, Ipswich

Elphinstone Primary School, Hastings

The Mary Erskine and Stewart's Melville Junior School,
Edinburgh

Lorne First School, Bradford

Bowling Park First School, Bradford

Aldwickbury School, Harpenden